How to Navigate Darkness

DW Gibbs

Published by DW Gibbs, 2017.

HOW TO NAVIGATE DARKNESS

First edition. December 31, 2017.

Written by DW Gibbs.

For Jill...

...simple as

Prologue

Let's start at the end. The end of me, to be precise. You see, the end of me is just the start of my story. I can barely recall the last five or so minutes of my life. When you drive as much as I did, you tend to zone out, letting your mind wander, leaving your sub-conscious to take to the wheel. How does the song go? There are fifty ways to leave your lover. Believe me, I had been searching for the right way, the right time, the right words. Maybe that is what was consuming me during those fateful minutes.

There is a vague retention of a truck snaking across the carriageway onto our side of the road, followed by an ardent light. Rising, yet the feeling of falling. Twisted chrome, weightlessness. Dispatched, subterranean unknowns. Plates and mantles displaced. Molten magma, obsidian. Bottomless. Then darkness. Pure, immaculate darkness.

'Our side of the road'. I was not travelling alone. My wife and two girls were in the car too, returning home after an unremarkable 4-day holiday in an unremarkable seaside town in southern New South Wales. Maybe it would have been more remarkable if I had managed to do the 'I'm leaving you' deed. Besides, if my wife hadn't loitered unnecessarily to fill in the 'visitor book' with faint, undeserved praise, then we would have left a truck-avoiding-death-inciting three minutes earlier.

This wasn't the way I wanted to leave her.

Such is life. And death.

====//====

"The most wasted day of all is that on which we have not laughed." – Nicolas Chamfort

He has them eating out of the palms of his hands. They may be clammy due to the 3-hour sweat-inducing hiatus since his last drink, but the mainly over-60s audience still respond to good jokes. "Knowing your audience is half the battle, sunshine", I heard him say to the chief purser earlier. The fact that he would probably never change his routine for any audience seems to be beside the point.

"I've been Jimmy Vince. Thank you for laughing. Good night, God bless"............. "Or maybe that should be.....I've been good. Thank God you for laughing. Bless Jimmy Vince......Ha Ha Ha!!.....Good night." One quick final wave, a wink of the eye and exit stage left to a not unreasonable amount of applause. Job done. Again.

This was the second performance I had seen of Jimmy Vince, a stand-up comedian from, I presume, the north of England. He was rather too old-school for my liking, eschewing the observational or satirical for up-and-down-the-line jokes. You know the sort, formal events about men going to the doctors or horses entering a bar. He obviously has an unending repertoire of material, as the hour I had just been subjected to contain none of the gags trotted out the night before.

Jimmy pours vodka into the tumbler that usually resides in the bathroom. There's an unmistakeable sheen of mouthwash still on the inside of the glass, turning the clear, neat alcohol into an opaque anti-sceptic cocktail. A vodka de menthe, please, barman. Not that Jimmy cares too much as he drowns the tumbler's contents. I'm guessing he's drunk much worse. The gentle sway of the boat helps to reinforce the effect of the vodka. There's a knock at the door.

"Enter", Jimmy shouts in his best Walter Matthau voice.

"Loved the one about the TVs getting married, Jimmy. You know, good reception. Nice one." A youngish man, probably in his mid-20's shuffles in and closes the door behind him.

"Ahh, the oldies are the goldies, young Adrian. Drink?"

"Why else do you think I came?" Adrian smiles. There are at least two or three more teeth than a human mouth should possess. He hands the glass he brought with him to Jimmy, seemingly aware of the perils of mouthwash. Glasses charged, they prop themselves up at either end of the lower deck of Jimmy's bunk bed. Muffled, but obviously raised voices emerge through the wall.

"Olga and Dimitri are at it again. She's a right mare. I hate Russian dolls........they're so full of themselves!"

"Boom boom."

And so the conversation starts. Gossip about the ship's crew. Who's sleeping with who. Shadowplay over, the point of reference switches again to comedy... the master and the apprentice, the jester and his muse. Adrian visited last night too, conversation lurching from tittle-tattle to tips. Jimmy is obviously happy to share, to sing from his hymn sheet of comedy how-to.

I share too, although I'm not really present in the room. I'm present in Jimmy. You see, Jimmy has been my host since I died on the road to Cann River. It seems that when I died, my mind and soul sank into the earth, directly passing through the earth's core, popping out at the precise antipode of my death.

I was lucky, it seems. At the precise moment I 'antipoded', Jimmy was lying in his cabin – on the floor where he'd passed out the night before after tangling with his liquefied Polish nemesis. If I had died 10 seconds later or the Santa Arena cruise ship had not left Ponta Delgada on time, then I would not have found my host and my journey to discover the truth would have been a very lame non-runner. Heaven, it seems, really is a place on earth. No angels manning pearly gates, just a hangover, loud flatulence and a severe case of bad breath.

I access my host's memories through a labyrinth of neural tunnels. Most of the tunnels are lit; some are dim; plenty are dark; and a few almost impregnable due to their blackness. It is the 'tunnel noir' that holds the memories that either have been purposely forgotten or the secrets that refuse to be aired. A truth never to be told. Since I entered Jimmy, I have worked out many things. I use his eyes for clues, for what he sees, I see. And then I travel his memories.

I have explored the hazy moments before my gatecrashing his rather solitary, drunken party. I have encountered a myriad of jokes, seemingly married to the twin temptresses of laughter and applause. I have taken the coast road of memories to childhood holidays in rainy seaside resorts in what looked like the North of England. I have bumped into a few adolescent petty crimes, one particular crime of passion and quite a number of crimes against fashion. So, halfway along G-deck, in the third cabin from the fire exit resides Jimmy Vince. For this small 105-night bracket in the long paragraph of the ship's history, it belongs to him, the cruise comedian. And me, of course.

There are less than two days left of the cruise before the Santa Arena returns to Southampton and Jimmy sits alone in his cabin memorising the final night's material. Pages of foolscap invade the unmade bed. Each page has a number relating to a specific day's setlist of jokes. Repeating a gag, even if it was from a fortnight ago is against his rules. In the near 15 weeks that Jimmy has been on the cruise he has delivered 89 half-hour sets, the ninetieth ahead of us tonight. Sheet 90 is Jimmy's tour de force, all his favourite material congregated for his last hurrah of this cruise. He sits at his wall-side formica desk, scanning the scribbled list of jokes, occasionally mouthing a punchline. There are words everywhere with interconnecting lines drawn on in red and capital letters in green ink to signify whole gags stripped back to handful of words and letters.

Jimmy stands up, turns to the mirror on the opposite wall and smiles. He holds the smile for a second or two.

"The doctor said to me... *I've got very bad news. You've got cancer and Alzheimer's.*" Straight face.

"I said.... *'well, at least I don't have cancer!'*" Another smile, bigger this time. He pauses, drinking in the imaginary applause, then ticks off the green CAPS of DOC.C&A from Sheet 90.

I am intrigued by his methods of remembering the order of the jokes. At least I think there is a specific order, a journey of mirth he wants the audience to follow, not dissimilar to a DJ's mixset creating some kind of symbiotic relationship with the listener. There seem to be over a hundred trigger words and phrases written on the flip side of Sheet 90. At first glance, random words pop out at me. A more detailed look reveals a rambling and incoherent short story with key words highlighted along the way. It begins with...... A baker has a beef with a skeleton....

Again, Jimmy stands and faces the mirror. That familiar smile.

"My baker has stopped making doughnuts." Pause.

"He's got tired of the hole thing." A nod accompanies the smile this time.

"What's the difference between roast beef and pea soup?" Eyebrows up, as if waiting for a response.

"Anyone can roast beef...." Smirk, pause, big smile, perfectly timed for when the audience realise the payoff.

He moves half a step closer to the mirror, as if he is on the verge of telling everyone a massive secret. Hand resting on top of the invisible microphone stand, he leans in even closer. This secret will be intimate, the most satisfying kind. He imagines the audience leaning in to listen.

"A skeleton walks into a bar." Half pause.... "and orders a beer." Half pause again..... "and a mop".

The next two and a half hours pass by in a blur of punchlines, pauses and smiles. Alternating between Sheet 90 on the desk and the mirror on the opposite wall, the time passes quickly. At first I find the whole mirror thing disconcerting, not only because I can actually see what my host looks like, but also due to the fact that, in essence, I am looking at me and what I have become. Jimmy is pale, pasty and slightly overweight – ironically, almost the complete opposite of me, as if being dragged through the earth's core to the exact opposite point of my death has turned me into a true antipode.

Whoever said that opposites attract is some kind of fool. Ignoring the fact that I hardly know the man and in spite of the obvious dedication to his craft, I am finding it difficult to warm to my host. He is, as far as I can ascertain, a drunk and a loser. I trawl through some more memories, hoping to dredge up something favourable from the canals in his brain rather than an abandoned shopping trolley or an old boot. There is definitely an ex-partner lurking in the neural maze. She appears in a number of tunnels, some light but most dark. He seems to want to forget about her or maybe the drink is turning the dimmer switch in his mind. Maybe the bottle has replaced her as his lover. But there are obviously some things that can never be assigned to oblivion, memories that cannot be rubbed out. They will remain with him forever. I hope that they do not haunt him. I would never wish that on anyone. Besides, haunting him seems to be my job at this moment in time.

I have no idea whether he is aware of my presence inside him. I do not even understand if or how my inhabitation can influence his behaviour or thoughts. I will learn these things over time. All I know is that I need to get back, to return to my family. They will need someone to watch over them.

====//====

Jimmy throws some water over his face and some mouthwash around his mouth. Spitting the contents into the basin, he checks the time on his comedy alarm clock. The doughnut-with-a-bite-out-of-it timepiece shows five minutes to midday, perfect timing for the descent into the ship's bowels to attend the midday disembarkation meeting which is compulsory for all the crew (according to the staff cruise itinerary which Jimmy checked earlier). It soon becomes apparent that Jimmy doesn't much care for the meeting as he spends the majority of it shut-eyed and heavy-breathed. I pick my way through the under-growth of his mind once more to find memories of an identical get-together on a previous cruise. Same room, same ennui, different people.

Jimmy wakes to the choir of chairs being pushed back, meeting over. He catches the eye of a grinning Adrian who puts his hand over his mouth, feigning a yawn. That boy really should do something about those teeth, especially if he wants to enter showbusiness rather than the circus. Jimmy mouths something and Adrian nods. I expect a departing masterclass is on the cards on the heels of tonight's final performance. Jimmy makes his way up two levels, responding to at least three passenger waves with a nod and a wink.

Lunchtime in the Four Seasons is a chaotic affair. Passengers swarm around the central buffet bar. Argy-bargy over culinary mediocrity. An errant meatball is crushed underfoot by an open-toed sandal amongst the waltzing throng forming a scrum over the vol-au-vents. Jimmy grabs a bowl of chow mein and ignores the chopsticks, instead grabbing a fork from next to the fruit platter.

Something is troubling Jimmy. Call it a sixth sense, or maybe it is me that is Jimmy's sixth sense. Whatever it is, it is giving me the dead body equivalent of a headache. He opens his cabin door and rushes over to the bed where Sheet 90 still lies. The incoherent story is having an overhaul. He strikes a line through the last three prompts, replacing "typewriting grasshoppers on Noah's Ark" to "Fred at the vets on a piano!!" There's something final about the whole thing, the double exclamation mark emphasising some kind of climax. He takes a bottle of vodka from the recess under the sink and decants some into a glass. He lets out a deep sigh and perches on the bottom bunk, hunched over, head lowered. My view of the cabin floor becomes blurred as his tears begin to form and then roll down his face, dripping onto his shoes. I feel helpless, not knowing what is causing the tears and not knowing if or how I can help.

Memories fizz and crackle. There are new ones coming to the forefront of his mind, many I had not explored before. Most are of life on the ship, from the highs of the nightly applause to the lows of the seemingly omnipresent morning hangovers and even some of the glorious tedium in between. There is even a flash of memory of being slapped across the face by a bus-conductor blonde at a staff party in amongst the emotional debris.

Another memory starts to form. Bright sunlight scintillates through the trees' canopies. Trembling, half-naked on the forest floor. We are snapped out the memory by a knock at the door. Narrowly missing smashing his head on the bunk above, Jimmy jumps up and throws water on his face, concealing the obvious saline tracks. Adrian pokes his dentally-challenged face around the cabin door. As I predicted, he is here for one last mentoring session before the cruise hits its final port of call.

Jimmy flicks through his CD wallet slowly, his finger like a metronome on valium. He finally finds the disc he wants, places it into his portable CD player and skips to the second track. There is a slight pause before the vocalist pierces the silence. Jimmy sings too....

"Do you fancy a drink, I know a place called the Brink. Do you wanna go there?"

Jimmy sways in the middle of the room, whilst Adrian makes himself comfortable at the away end of the bunk.

"I can buzz off your smile ....well, not yours, Ade....," Jimmy ad libs... *"and there may be people you know there".*

"This..." Jimmy points at the speaker... "this, my friend, is what those in the know call Northern Poetry".

"Who is it? I like it," Adrian leans forward.

"A genius by the name of John Bramwell and his band of merry men, I Am Kloot. Robbin' the rich to give the poor a little bit more northern soul." Jimmy seems pleased with himself. The song continues on a magic carpet ride of strings and yearning. Even I am enjoying its inevitable air of melancholy. Jimmy goes on.

"There's something about the north. You see, laughter and tears are never far apart in northern life"......which I find prescient, because that is all I have experienced since Jimmy became my host. His tears and other people's laughter. He charges Adrian's grateful glass and then, inevitably, his own.

"You know the difference between people from the north and south, Ade?"

"I'm sure you're just about to tell me, James."

"You see, you lot will joke about how you got one over on someone, but we'll joke about what a prick we've made of ourselves. We also are indebted to the past, a kind of nostalgia addiction, you know?" Jimmy continues, pointing his finger in Ade's direction. "Don't know who said it but it's bob on. Get this. When judging southerners we must always remember that they have not had the benefit of our disadvantages. How fookin' good is that?" Jimmy is on a roll now, directing the traffic of conversation down his one-way street.

"This song's about the brink. It's a boozer but it's really a metaphor for northern life, you know what I'm saying." Adrian nods. I'm sure he has no idea what Jimmy is saying.

"I wish I could articulate the juxtaposition of pathos and yearning as well as this fella. The brink, eh? What would you do, Ade, when you've reached the brink?"

"Err, I dunno." Adrian looks two-parts confused to one-part scared.

"You know, when you've had enough of yearning and want out. When you've done too much sailing down life's shit-filled canals. To end the pain. To end up tits up in a ditch." Ade's face is now all-parts scared. Jimmy edges closer and leans over Adrian, staring into his shocked eyes.

"Bang, bang. The only way, I reck. Quick as you like and very rock 'n' roll." Jimmy smiles and straightens up. A simple bassline fills the room.

"If heaven is a place upon your skin, that I may have touched from without to within. Well, then dust yourself for fingerprints and grin."

"Anyway, that's enough about me, what about you, Ade, my cockney sparrow?"

Adrian is still reeling, not quite sure where the conversation is going. He composes himself and looks earnest.

"This time next year, I'll be up there on stage doing my own thing, Jim. I really want it. So bad." His tone is serious and Jimmy joins him on the bed.

"Oh, you'll make it cocker. Keep listening to your Uncle Jimbo and you'll be as sound as a pound." Now it's serious face time from Jimmy.

"Reckon tonight's my last night." Jimmy mumbles, barely audible over the music.

"Well we *are* hitting Southampton tomorrow." Ade replies, trying to alleviate the gravitas of the comment.

"No, that's it, fella. No more cruises. Finito Benito."

Ade splutters a response, "Why? What's your plan? Who's going to be the cruise comic? Why? ....Why?"

"I'm tied in for another year. Two more bloody round-the-worlds. Duty-free can only numb the pain so much. I'm quitting."

Ade looks aghast. Those teeth on show again. "But they won't let you quit. You're.... you're... ," Ade struggles to find the words, "you're the man."

Jimmy shakes his head and fixes his eyes on Adrian's shocked expression.

"Einstein said that insanity is doing the same thing over and over again but expecting different results." Jimmy sighs and continues. "Me and the gags. Me and the booze. Me and this chuffin' ship. Sometimes, old son, the fountain runs shallow."

"But isn't this a great life? Doing what you want to do, what you do best, making people laugh." Adrian, almost pleading, shuffles on the bed.

"Listen, I try a little too hard, I drink a little too much. And I come back to this cold bed after the show and I think 'that was fine'. My life has become one long fucking line of fine." Adrian looks on, eyes wide.

"And I've started to hear voices."

====//====

I find this whole situation difficult to fathom. In life, I positioned myself somewhere between an atheist and an agnostic. In death, I do not know what to believe. This feels more like an afterthought than an afterlife. I spent the first day mourning, the fate of my family troubling me greatly and thinking about the wasted moments I had been at the helm of in my life. I wish I had done this more and that less. I wish I had lived every day like it was my last, especially that last day.

When did I last say that I loved them? Shit, I can't even remember. Despite spending a good proportion of my life trying to cultivate some 'me' time, I miss them. My soul aches for another hug, another game of sleeping lions or another eskimo kiss – the kind where you rub noses together and giggle at the silliness of it all. I miss sitting entwined around the fire pit, listening to the orchestra of cicadas sounding closer than they actually are, all playing the same notes, but never quite in the right order. I miss everyone's priceless smiles in photoframes, instances of happier times. I think I will always be thinking about what I am missing. In life, you look at what you have, not what you miss, and you move forward. In death, you look at what you don't have and what you miss. But you still have to move forward.

====//====

The start of Jimmy's set, which I was party to earlier is getting a pleasing reaction of titters and guffaws. He seems on edge, though, a simmering pot on the verge of coming to an almighty boil. And scalding someone. After the initial shock of inhabiting a cruise ship entertainer, this is the first time that I have felt truly uncomfortable. His confession about hearing voices disturbed me. I had not realised I could be heard, never mind affect him adversely. I thought I was only a silent partner in his joke-telling business.

The gags come thick and fast initially. Sheet 90's cryptic codes unveil themselves as crowd-pleasers, joke recipes that the audience find not only palatable, but downright tasty too. In the hours before tonight's performance there had been more changes to the coded script. A few trigger words had been moved from late in the piece to an earlier section and great swathes of words from the second half of the 'story' had been replaced altogether with new ones. This had left Jimmy with little time to prepare – surely the reason for his edginess – meaning frequent pauses were now starting to infiltrate his set.

"A man and a woman start to have sex in the middle of a dark forest. After about 15 minutes of it, the man finally gets up and says, "Bloody hell, I wish I had a torch!" The woman says, "Me too, you've been eating grass for the past ten minutes!" About half the audience laugh, but there's an audible gasp from some and a solitary tut. Jimmy loosens his collar and presses on. Profanities start to litter Jimmy's material. There's a 'Fuck', a couple of 'shits" and plenty of other swear words. The audience is turning – this is not the jovial mirth-maker they have been used to for nigh on 15 weeks. A few have already stood up and walked out and there are now people heckling him.

"OK, OK, it's time for me to sign off. But remember, there's no such thing as bad language, only bad use of good language. I've been Jimmy Vince and I'll leave you lucky people with ***the*** greatest gag in the world. Ever. Good night and God bless." Jimmy wanders to the far right hand side of the stage and turns on his heels to face the crowd. He breathes deeply and launches into his final joke of the evening (the one described as 'piano' on Sheet 90).

"A man walks in the poshest hotel restaurant in all of London town. "*Where's the goddam, mother-fucking manager, you cock-sucker?*", he asks the nearest waiter."

[I see an elderly couple rise and edge their way to the exit]

"The waiter is naturally taken aback and replies, "*Excuse me sir, could you please refrain from using that sort of language in here. I will get the manager straight away.*" The manager comes over and the man says, " *Are you the fucking manager of this bastard joint?*"

[More gasps and another retiree from the audience, but Jimmy is relentless]

"*Yes, I am the manager, but I would prefer if you didn't use language like that.*"

"*Piss off,*" the man gesticulates, "*where's the fucking piano?*"

"*Ahhh, you've come about the pianist job,*" the manager sighs and shows him over to the piano, "*can you play any blues?*" The man sits at the piano and plays THE most inspiring and heartfelt honky-tonk blues that the manager has ever heard.

"*That was amazing! What's it called?*" the manager asks.

"*I want to screw your wife on the settee, but my cock's sore.*"

[More movement and a general low murmur rises from the audience]

The manager is somewhat disturbed and asks the man if he knows any jazz. The man proceeds to play the most melancholic jazz piece the manager has ever heard. "Magnificent! What's that called?" cries the manager.

"*As I wank under the stars with the moonlight shining off my bell-end,*" replies the man.

[Some people in ship uniform appear at the back of the auditorium and one of them motions with his hand across his throat. He wants Jimmy to stop. Unsurprisingly, Jimmy carries on]

"The manager is highly offended but offers him the job on the condition that he doesn't introduce any of his songs or talks to the customers.

This arrangement works well for a few weeks until one night, sitting opposite him is the most beautiful blonde he has ever laid his eyes on. She's wearing an almost see-through dress, her legs are slightly open and she is sucking suggestively on an asparagus spear with butter dripping down her chin."

[A woman in the front row faints. Jimmy doesn't falter]

"The man has to disappear to the toilet to 'relieve' himself when he hears the manager asking where the pianist is. He just has time to shoot his bolt and in a fluster, he runs back to the piano having not bothered to adjust himself properly, sits down and starts playing again."

[Two crew members in full ship regalia are now climbing onto the stage and are heading towards Jimmy]

"The blonde steps up to the piano, leans over and whispers in his ear."

"*Do you know your cock and balls are hanging out of your trousers and dripping jizz on your shoes?*"

"The man replies, "*Know it? .... I fucking wrote it!*""

====//====

I remember sitting in church as a small child, my brother, Michael, and I flanking my mother. Dad would never enter the joint, which comes as no surprise, really. I remember it being an imposing place, the vaulted ceiling stretching all the way to heaven, it seemed. Angels, cavorting in the oversized windows, illuminated the whole place. There had to be clouds up there in the rafters too, maybe even God and his eternal wrath, looking down at me and my brother, judging and planning his punishment for us.

But the thing about church was, well, nothing actually happened. Ever. Our Reverend, a kindly, but solemn man named Pritchard never once took up residence on the spiritual high ground and preached anything. He merely rocked up and mumbled his way through his sermon, pausing briefly to half-heartedly sing a psalm or two along the way. It wasn't like there was a lot of spiritual intervention going on in real life either. Just by looking at the daily news, it was fairly obvious that God was getting even less involved than Rev Pritchard.

====//====

Another SNAFU sunrise. Jimmy leans over the guard rail on the upper deck, drawing in the fresh morning air. If this doesn't clear his head, nothing will. Last night was very instructive for me. For one, I learnt a lot more about my host and, what's more, a whole lot about me and my new 'life'. Jimmy has been fired from his job on the cruise ship. There were 29 complaints (and counting) about the content of his set – a ship record, apparently. Not that Jimmy cares, as that was his objective all along. Quitting, it seems, was never on the agenda (not part of his creative ethos...... Ha!), so getting fired was the least worst option........ "proper rock 'n' roll way to go" as Jimmy put it at the crew party last night. Whereas Jimmy is suffering (yet again) from a hangover, I am feeling altogether much more up-beat. I have found a way out. A way home.

How can I describe the act of transmigration, this transition through the act of touching from one body to another? I'm not sure language is enough because sometimes language cannot read the music of meaning or express the thrill of hope.

It all happened during the unseemly melee at the end of Jimmy's show. The important-looking crew members in epaulets were frog-marching Jimmy off stage when I experienced a juddering surge of neural energy. Imagine a vertical drop with a smooth polished runway. You close your eyes, cross your arms and ease yourself over the edge. And then you somehow end up in the body (mind, to be precise) of the person your host is touching. Of course, I had no idea what was going on and panicked, reversing the transmigration process and returning back to Jimmy.

So, it seems that I am free to travel despite being trapped in a neural nightmare. I have to plan my escape, pick my new host and plot my way home somehow. I have no idea how long it will take or how arduous the journey may be, but I need, need, need to find out what happened to the others. I have an inherent objective now, a purpose in death, unlike in my life which ambled along with little to no purpose.

Southampton looms into view later that morning. It seems bigger than I had imagined. There are five cruise ships already in the huge harbour, giant alien swans that have invaded the village duckpond. England in October is a big grey canvas. Anonymous people swarm under angry skies. There is a storm brewing. In more ways than one. Jimmy's mood seems darker than the sky. Does he regret last night's actions now? There is a maelstrom of thoughts swirling through his mind at the moment.

Jimmy is escorted off the boat before the passengers and their luggage are scheduled to disembark. He wheels his suitcase (surprisingly small) across the quayside, turns briefly, sticks two fingers up to the Santa Arena and heads towards the town centre. He dives into one of those ubiquitous high street mobile phone shops and buys £20-worth of credit for his phone which, looking at it, can barely be described as mobile. If Jimmy looks like he's been around the block a bit, then his phone has bought the t-shirt.

Four doors down from the phone shop is a pub. Without breaking stride, Jimmy swings open the door, his case catching in it. He yanks it clear and enters the empty establishment, shouting to the landlord.

"Pint of Best, cocker. And a vodka chaser." He seems in no mood for conversation and the landlord obliges him, lining up the drinks in silence. Jimmy throws a ten-pound note on the bar. Retiring to a long bench in the far back corner of the bar, Jimmy drowns half of his pint and takes his phone out. His thumb hits the down button and a list of names appear on the screen. He scrolls down to "Vern" and presses the green 'dial' button.

- Vernon Goddard, Agent to the stars

- Guess who's back in town, Big Vern?

- Well, stone them crows. James Vince as I live and breathe.

- Well recognised.

- You're the only northern monkey who works for me, Jimmy! Of course I recognised you.

- You work for me, you cheeky brummie bastard. And don't you forget it. I'm head of your entertainment portfolio.

There's a bellow of laughter down the line – the first Jimmy has had since about half way through last night's show. He seems grateful.

- What have you got for me, Vern?

- Didn't expect you back til tomorrow at the earliest. How do you fancy a bit of student action?

- I was rather hoping for the Palladium or the Royal Albert Hall.

I was rather hoping for an Australian tour, if truth be told.

- Got a 5-night Fresher's week university tour.

- You've got to be jokin'.

- You're the joker, remember. It's the "Mirth, Magic and Memories" tour.

- The what?

- Ivan Illusion does the magic. 8-Ties do 80's covers, that's the memories bit. And you, apparently, do the mirth.

- How much?

- Just say you'll do it.

- How much?

- Err, three hundred.

- Per show? OK, done deal. Job's a good 'un.

There's a lengthy pause. Jimmy skulls the vodka shot.

- Listen, I've got to go, Jimmy. Err, drop in tomorrow. The gigs start next week. Bye.

- Cheers, Vern. TTFN.

The line goes dead before he finishes his goodbyes. Jimmy looks at his phone and shakes his head. He gives off an aura of disappointment. Surely, beggars can't be choosers, especially after last night's carry on. Leaving the half-drained pint on the table, Jimmy wheels his case into the toilets. There are three cubicles set off to the right, with a metal urinal trough opposite. Jimmy slips into the middle cubicle, squeezing his case in with him. He stands on the toilet seat, reaches up to dislodge the polystyrene tile directly above the cistern, then fumbles blindly in the dark void. A plastic bag emerges from the blackness and a smile breaks out on Jimmy's face.

"Fookin' bingo! Market day," he whispers, jumping down off the seat. He fishes inside the bag and hooks out a battered tobacco tin. Sitting on the toilet seat, Jimmy snaps open the lid and pops one of its treasures, something wrapped in a cigarette paper, into his mouth. He returns the tin to the bag and stuffs it into the front flap of his case.

Back in the lounge bar, the remainder of his beer is used to help swallow his oral cargo and Jimmy sits back and sighs deeply, allowing the pub's country and western music to provide the soundtrack to his wait. Of all the bars, in all the towns, my host had to pick this one. I need to get out of this guy.

====//====

Jimmy is pretty high when Adrian makes his appearance at the pub. Rat-a-tat conversation at breakneck speed seems the order of the day. Jimmy is spewing random thoughts and provocative opinions in equal measure and I have no choice but to ride the rollercoaster. Adrian struggles to be part of any kind of two-way conversation, as Jimmy's amphetamines take further hold. The afternoon races by fuelled by vodka and speed. Adrian eats the house-special 'pork pie & piccalilli'. Jimmy plumps for his personal 'tasting menu', dining alone in cubicle number 2. The conclusion to the afternoon's verbal one-way street is a decision to catch the 1548 train to London Victoria and then on to Adrian's parents' house in Dagenham, where it's agreed that Jimmy will stay until his mini-tour kicks off.

Whilst Adrian exchanges small talk with the landlord, Jimmy hits the toilet for one last time. Again he squeezes his case into the cubicle and gets the tobacco tin out again. "One for the road," he mutters as his index finger dabs the white crystalline powder. He returns the tin to the plastic bag and I catch a glimpse of what else the bag holds. Even in the dim, blue fluorescent light, it is unmistakable, the metal of the barrel managing a glint, especially for me. Even in the dim, blue fluorescent light, it is obvious that Jimmy has a gun.

====//====

I had thought it started with the slap across my face. But, in truth, it had started way before then. Maybe I should have rolled over, returned to one of those dreams that never reach the end. Maybe if I had I would not have breached the levee of blame. A blame laid like mortar. Thick and permanent. 3am and there is an empty space where my wife should have been sleeping next to me. Noises emanate from the garden so I get up to investigate. A shadowy silhouette on the lawn. Unmistakably my wife. Shoulders uncontrollable, face down, wailing, arms out. It is a vision which violates the heart, a vision of utter sorrow, so profound, so remediless. A vision of a woman looking down at her empty arms. A place where our son should have been. A place where he would never be now. A place where I could never be anymore.

====//====

It is dark when we arrive at the two-up, two-down terraced house in East London. Adrian introduces Jimmy to his parents, Alan and Veronica, who usher us in to the front room. Their home seems to be a shrine to self-help amid an altar of kitsch. Signs and messages adorn the walls, whilst brass horseshoes and porcelain animals inhabit the mantelpiece and dresser.

Jimmy, heart still racing, points and reads aloud the motto from one of the canvas prints on the wall.

"Think big and dream bigger. Too true, Alan, too true." He then mutters under his breath, "Ready, set, pull the trigger."

Veronica gives Adrian an enveloping hug and lets off a huge sigh, "Thank God you're home safe, Ade. You know how I worry. Now, who's for a lovely cuppa?"

Nods of assent from Alan and Adrian.

"Oooh, yes please, Veronica," from Jimmy.

"Call me Ronnie, James."

"Call me Jimmy, Ron." Jimmy winks. Ronnie wanders off into the kitchen giggling.

Alan stretches out in his armchair and motions for Jimmy to sit down on the sofa. He and Adrian bookend the rather jaded 1970's chamois-brown leather 3-seater. Adrian practically disappears into it, while Jimmy prefers to perch on its edge.

"Now then Alan. Ade has told me next to nothing about you." I can feel Adrian blushing. "What do you do?"

"I work at the plant, you know the car factory down the road. I'm a Union man." It seems Alan is more than happy to engage in conversation.

"I'm betting that you're a Labour man, Jimmy. You've got the voice for it!"

"Well, uh, yeah, suppose I am. I'm not that political though, Alan. Mind you, I've done a few demonstrations in my time. You know, marching and the like. Poll tax, teachers, nurses gigs, supporting the miners back in the day." Jimmy goes on, "It's our God-given right to protest. Suffering in silence makes cowards of you and me, Alan." Jimmy has lit the fuse.

"That's the spirit, Jimmy! I'm a Union man and even with all of their faults, trade unions have done more for humankind than any other organisation of men that ever existed. You see throughout the years, they've done more for honesty, for decency, for education…. ," Alan shifts forward in his seat and continues, "…for the betterment of us as human beings than any other association of men."

"And women!!" Ronnie shouts from the kitchen.

"Yes dear, and women," Alan raises his eyebrows. "In fact it was down the road at the Ford factory that women machinists went on strike to get equal pay. If it wasn't for them, and Ronnie's dear mother was one of 'em, there'd be no Equal Pay Act of 1970."

"Christ, you know your stuff, Alan."

"I just want what's right for people, because if you don't stand for something you'll fall for anything!"

Ronnie walks in with four cups of tea on a tray and offers Jimmy one first.

"Oh, Alan, leave the poor lad alone. He's only been 'ere five minutes."

Now it is the turn of Jimmy to hold court. He talks breathlessly of how joke-telling is becoming a lost art form, how Adrian has been learning from him and why he should be given the cruise comedian gig. Moreover, Jimmy is going to tell them, no implore them, to hire Adrian for the next season. And what of Jimmy, Ronnie asks. For the first time in what seems like forever, Jimmy hesitates and goes quiet.

"Dunno, I'll find something," he mumbles. "Where's your toilet?"

Alan pipes up again. "That's the spirit, Jimmy! Remember, each man is the architect of his own fate because fate leads the willing and drags along the reluctant. First door on the left." But Jimmy is already halfway down the corridor, willingly making his own fate.

====//====

"Are you alright?" Alan and Veronica have gone to bed and Adrian seems worried about Jimmy.

"Yeah, why?" Jimmy's heart is still beating twenty-to-the-dozen.

"Dunno. You seem on edge tonight. Well, all day, if I'm honest."

Jimmy IS on edge. Amphetamines and calmness don't often party together.

"Don't you think I've got an excuse to be a bit, you know, edgy about things? I've just lost my job remember." Jimmy's voice hardens.

"You pretty much jacked it in, though, Jim. Besides, you'll be alright. You've got that tour starting next week. And there's bound to be other stuff."

"The 'Mirth, Magic and Memories' bollocks is hardly gonna set me up for life, is it?"

I know this for a fact as I saw a text message earlier to Jimmy from Vernon highlighting that the £300 stated was for the whole tour and not per night. Jimmy inhales and crumples up his face.

"Life is a series of disappointments, cocker, broken only by sporadic spells of darkness. And sometimes, just sometimes, the darkness gets so dark, you know like when the sky gets really, really black and you know it's gonna piss it down. And you wait for that first lightning bolt and thunderclap. And you know it's comin', that first crack in the darkness and the storm is officially allowed to start and there's no going back...." Jimmy is babbling now. Breathe, Jimmy, breathe.

"There's no going back, Ade, there's no going back......." He tails off mid-sentence, the words left hanging in the air waiting for a reaction, to be shot down or rescued. But nothing comes and we're left with the silence of that nothing, drowned out by the deafening noise of the threat.

====//====

It is the middle of the night and we are still staring at the ceiling. Jimmy cannot sleep and, as a consequence, I cannot switch off either. It can be quite tiring existing in this state of flux I can tell you. When his eyes finally close, I go in search of more answers in his mine of memories. I need to dig even deeper than before to get a handle on Jimmy's darkness. There must be something, or someone maybe, buried deep in here that is the root of his angst. I dive in. There seem to be "no entry" signs at every neural twist and turn, barriers to entry wrapped up tightly in red tape. Eventually, in an isolated REM moment, I find a way in.

The leaves are burnished brown and there is a heady smell of lavender in the air (did I mention that memories secrete smells too?!). A bigger body is on top of Jimmy and the scent of lavender and damp leaves is replaced by the whiff of fear. Fumbling and fear arm-wrestle in the late summer air. What appears to be a teenage fight becomes something altogether more sinister. Whilst Jimmy is obviously young, the stronger body gaining the upper-hand on top is not. Body odour and stubble. Stale beer and panting. He claws at the young Jimmy, muttering threats......"stay still".........."it won't hurt".........."our secret".........

Jimmy stops fighting, succumbing, doors open for violation, face down in the leaves. The sobbing stops, eventually, but only when the predator has released his prey. He comes close again. "Not a fuckin' word, Vince." He pulls up his long khaki shorts and adjusts his neckerchief and woggle.

"Can't hear you, Vince." The sobs start again.

Louder this time, "Can't fuckin' hear you!" Jimmy's voice is unbroken and full of fear.

"Akela, we'll....*sniff*...... do our...*sob*.....best."

"That's better." The man breathes into Jimmy's ear and walks off through the woods.

I shudder and Jimmy wakes with a start.

"What the fuck was *that*?!?" he gasps, our eyes, once again, trained on the once-white Artex ceiling.

====//====

Your toy balloon has sailed in the sky, love.
But now it must fall to the ground.
Now your sad eyes reveal, just how badly you feel.
'Cause there is no easy way down.

The view from the cliffs must have been exciting.
And up to the peaks, you were bound.
Now you're stranded alone and the past is unknown.
And there is no easy way down.

No it isn't very easy, when you're left on your own.
No it isn't very easy, when each road you take is one
more mistake.

There's no-one to break your fall and lead you back home.

We all like to climb to the heights of love,
Where our fantasy world can be found.
But you must know in the end, when it's time to descend,
There is no easy way down.
You know you're gonna find, there is no easy way down.

Jimmy's handwriting is a little neater than usual. He folds the piece of paper twice and thrusts it into his jacket pocket. Alan appears from the kitchen with a tray of bacon sandwiches.

"'Ere you go, Jimbo, get yer laughing gear round that," Alan puts the serving tray on the dining table and motions to Jimmy. "You must be starving. You've eaten next to nothing since you got here."

"Thanks, Alan, much obliged." Jimmy reaches for the HP Sauce and flips open the lid. He goes on, "bet you don't know why it's called HP Sauce, Al?"

Alan shrugs, "I've absolutely no idea."

Jimmy lets out a snort as he squirts the brown sauce onto his opened sandwich.

"It's staring you in the face!"

"What is?"

"The answer, Alan. What can you see?" Alan moves nearer to the table.

"A ruddy big clock. Big Ben, innit?"

"Bloody hell fire, Alan. It's the Houses of Parliament. Houses of Parliament Sauce, cocker." Jimmy takes an enormous bite out of the sandwich.

"Well I never. 'Ere, Ronnie, come 'ere a sec," Alan shouts into the kitchen.

By the time Alan has gone through the exact same HP rigmarole, Jimmy has polished off his second sandwich and is finishing packing his case. We are off into London to see Big Vern. Well, that's what the text Jimmy received earlier said.

"C U @ 11 my office. More on tour 4 u. V".

Who knows, maybe I can fit a spot of transmigration in too. After all, today is one day closer to my kind of tomorrow.

====//====

Jimmy is already running late for his meeting with Vern. Protracted goodbyes with Adrian, Alan and Veronica, coupled with an unsurprisingly tardy journey into London – points failure at Mile End, passenger setting off an alarm at Bow and Jimmy taking the wrong fork at Piccadilly Circus – means it is nearer midday when we arrive at Vern's third floor office. Multiple flights of stairs don't help Jimmy's somewhat beclouded mood. He pauses outside the office door, a big mahogany affair with a gold-plated plaque centre stage.

Vernon Goddard - Commercial, Theatrical & Talent Agent

Jimmy raps his knuckles just under the sign.

"Knock Knock."

"Who's there?" booms the reply from inside.

"Theodore."

"Theodore who?"

Jimmy opens the door and pokes his head around it, feigning an over-the-top Italian accent. "Theodore wasn't open so I a-knocked."

"Come in, you northern schmuck."

"Y'all right, cock?"

"Better than you, I'm guessing. What happened to the Alpha Cruises gig?"

"Let's call it a misunderstanding. I'm free as a bird now." Jimmy sits down in a hoary armchair. The office reeks of old Havana, the source of which is a mountain of corona blunts in a cavernous ashtray. I spy Vern through the malodorous haze.

"A misunderstanding? I heard you nearly got yourself arrested."

"Yeah, absolute scenes," Jimmy says, with more than a hint of pride in his voice.

"Listen, Jimmy, since I've been sat here waiting for you to finally arrive," Vern looks at his computer screen, "I've had the sum total of six emails. One is from my ex-wife asking for more allowance, another is from some geezer trying to flog me Viagra." Jimmy chuckles. Vern doesn't. "And four, yes four, are asking about Pascoe's availability. The grand total of emails related to James Bernard Vince?" Vern doesn't wait for an answer. "Zero, none, zilch, nada, or to be blunt," he pauses for effect, "fuck all."

"Give over. Yeah, well, maybe you haven't actually told 'em of my availability. Everyone must think I'm tied up with projects and stuff. You've got to communicate, Vern. Talk to them. Chuffin' plead, if you have to."

"Listen already. Really listen." Vern cups his ear dramatically and looks up to the ceiling.

"What?"

"What can you hear?"

"Nothing."

"Yeah, that's the only communication I ever hear from you, sunshine."

"Well, I've been a bit, well, incommunicado, haven't I?"

"Well, so have the booking agents, big man."

"What's Pascoe got lined up, then?"

"Practically a whole national tour, plus a possible night at the Palladium."

"What, *the* Palladium?"

"Yes, Jimmy, the very same."

"Why not me? Get on the blower, Vern. Do your job for once."

Vern sighs heavily and raises his palms to the ceiling.

"I'll tell you why not you, James Vince. You're still doing the same straight up and down shit you always did. With Pascoe and Vince it fitted with the times. Your timing was great. You had a beguiling ease together. You could even finish..."

"...each other's sentences," Jimmy bristles a little as he speaks, "I know."

"You were good together. You were a double act. But shit happens, Jimmy."

"Yeah, I thought we had one of those unspoken relationships, like we knew what each other was thinking. And then one day, he fucked off. The one thing I didn't expect him to be thinking."

A silence finally pervades the room. I scan the office and then retreat into Jimmy's recesses. I need a rest from their tennis match banter.

I slide into Jimmy's time machine and decide to hunt for his old comedy partner, Pascoe, as I don't seem to have come across him yet.

We all have our own time machines. Memories, good and bad, occupy the rear-view mirror. Only dreams take us forward in our time machines, seen through the portal of the front windscreen. Some windscreens are huge and some offer limited visibility. Jimmy's windscreen is modest, fogged up, and has a sizable crack meandering across it. I resurface to dead air. Vern exhales loudly and breaks the lull.

"Anyway, Clem's changed, he's adapted. His satirical stuff is sensational. You heard it? He even does improv in his set. It'd scare the shit out of me."

"Doubt it. You were always good at making it up as you go along." Jimmy mutters, audibly.

"Point is, Jim, in this business you need to evolve or die. At the moment, you're heading the same way as the dinosaurs."

"Eff off, Vern. 'Scuse my manc."

"You're excused."

There is a stifling smog inside Jimmy's head. A pea-souper of a downer freshly mixed with stale cigar smoke. It is hard to see anything, nothing is clear. I'm surprised Jimmy can function at all.

"So where's the first gig, then?"

"The New University."

"The New University?"

"Yeah, one of those old Polytechnics. It's now a Uni."

"Couldn't they think of a better name? Any famous old students waste three years of their lives there, back in the day?"

"Obviously not, Jim. Although I do know that the Green Cross Code Man lived down the road from there once. Does that count?" Vern lets out a huge belly-laugh.

"Anyway, three hundred sheets for the whole tour? You're taking the piss. Snide bastards."

"Actually, it's them that are taking the piss and giving you a job, all at the same time. I thanked them and so should you," Vern remarks, smugly.

"Chuff off."

"Look Jimmy," Vern attempts to appease his troublesome client, "why don't you try some new material, maybe some observational stuff? It's all the rage. You observe, don't you? Use these gigs as a new start, a trial run. Some good reviews and you're off and running again."

"Observation? But I'm known for my jokes. I tell jokes, I'm a not an effin' philosopher." Jimmy returns fire.

"All I know is that almost everything is best when it's about something. Use the gags to shed some light on you. You know, the human condition. That's the truth, right there." Vern points his unlit cigar in Jimmy's direction.

"My condition is hardly a laugh a minute."

"Give it a try, already," Vern harangues.

"I'll give you some chuffin' truths, Vernon. As a comic, it's all about you. They don't not like your material or what you look like or what you're wearing," Jimmy stands up and goes on. "They just don't like *you*. It's about as personal as it can possibly get. Opening the can of truths about yourself, well, it'll make things worse. I want laughs, not bloody sympathy." Jimmy is already heading for the door.

"At least have a think about it. Promise me that," Vern says matter-of-factly, returning to a pile of paperwork bidding for attention on his desk.

"Seeking approval by bloody proxy. From chuffin' strangers. I must be mad." Jimmy heads for the door. Without looking up, Vern replies, "there'll be material in that madness, if you look hard enough."

Jimmy gives Vern a flick of the 'V's and we dissolve into London's frenetic, slate-grey afternoon.

I wonder if my funeral has taken place as it has been almost a week since my death. Would it have been just my funeral or a requiem for the whole family? I didn't sense anybody else lurking inside others on the boat, but maybe they didn't die at the scene and the antipodal shift was an impossibility.

I also wonder how many people would have turned up. I think of old friends drinking in my memory, new acquaintances wishing they had known me longer, children running around questioning what all the fuss is about. And I think of the music. Did I mention my death playlist in a drunken haze to anybody? Will the congregation be wiping a tear away to Eva Cassidy's "Autumn Leaves" or inhaling Tom Hickox's exquisite lament "Let me be your Lover"? Planning for the saddest day in somebody else's life is such a great joy. I only wish I could be there myself. And then there is the disconsolate figure shrouded in black, where there are no words, only sobbing. And when the song of life ends, you hope that at least the melody lingers on.

But the reality will be far different. Few friends turn up and then spend the hour checking the time on their mobile phones intermittently; solemn hymns fill the air irking the sceptics; there will be vain repetitions of the Lord's Prayer more akin to the heathens than the heavens; and the few that do wish to celebrate your life will be turfed out of the pub because the relief barman hasn't shown up and the bar tab has long since run dry.

D.H. Lawrence said that the dead don't die, they look on and help. I look on, from afar, and I certainly cannot help. Well, not yet. It may take forever, but I will get back and look on and help. Problem is, forever is not really knowing.

====//====

"Evolve or die." Jimmy repeats Vern's mantra as he shuffles towards the oversize mirror in the motel room.

"News is never good news. Always bad. Makes you wonder whether it's worth getting out of bed and moisturizing." He waits for a couple of seconds, allowing the words to form before setting them loose.

"It was always the 3 S's in the morning – shit, shower and shave. With the news the way it is, I'm going to have to turn into Sean Connery – shit, shower and shave the world."

Jimmy shakes his head.

"Fookin' terrible."

"OK, here we go again. Let's try this. Observe, James, observe."

A clearing of the throat and he's away, "I got a cat, to keep me company. You know, a little bundle of fluff to come home to every night. It hated me. Went to the animal doctor.... Oh, shit....I mean I went to the vet and he said to get it spayed. So I did. And pause, wait for it. And go." Jimmy leans in to the mirror, like a church booth's confessional hole.

"So I bought a fookin' spade. Very good advice from the man. Lots of uses...you can kill the little shit with it and then use it to dig a hole to bury the selfish bastard in afterwards."

Jimmy waits for the imaginary applause, and when that fails to arrive, sighs and mutters, "Bobbins. Absolute bobbins."

"We're told it's a dog-eat-dog world out there. But when was the last time you saw a shih tzu nibble on a St Bernard? Oh, this is madness," he tails off, slamming his palm onto the desktop, sending the TV remote cascading to the carpet.

There'll be material in that madness, Jimmy

He bores into the mirror, glowering at his reflection. It's hard to reconcile he is addressing an audience, imaginary or otherwise, such is the intensity of the stare. He is accosting any-one who will listen, especially me.

"Have you any idea what it's like being a comic? Have you? It's not all laughs, I can tell you."

"Let me tell you. If you like constant travel, to be constantly moving, like some kind of fuckin' fugitive on the run, then this is the game for you. You get to hang out in cities where you know nobody. In fact, you're the first people I've actually spo-ken to all day! Apart from myself..........oh yeah, get used to that. Talking to yourself. All the time. Like some made-up, fake friend. Occasionally they talk back, well, mine does anyway. Do you think it's possible to mistake schizophrenia for ESP, I hear you ask?"

"It's OK, I'll wait," Jimmy does his raised-eyebrows-look-ing-at-his-watch face. "I'm here all week."

"Oh, and don't expect to be paid well. Even if you are, you've got to eat. And eating on the road is rough. I mean, look at me."

"Choose the fish and there'll be a black hole in your pay packet, hey?"

"All for a laugh. All for a fookin' laugh. I don't want a chufty badge or owt. From a standing ovation to complete si-lence in your mingin' hotel room...actually, I don't think I've ever had a standing ovation. I'm a Professor in fookin' silence, though. Ahh, scrap that bit."

There'll be material in that madness, Jimmy.

"Maybe there is some mileage in this kind of stuff, after all."

Jimmy looks down at the thin, shelf-like desk. His mono-grammed drug tin sits staring, no pleading, at him. He relents, pops the lid and fingers its crystal contents. Sucking the uppers off his digit, he focuses on the initials on the lid.

"JV. That's it. JV. Jimmy Vitriol. One for the fookin' ages. Vern will love that."

====//====

I wish I could go back and tell Maddy that everything will be OK. Go back to before the cracks appeared. That bassline fracture in our relationship seemed to appear one day and, like a chip in a windscreen, it started to break apart bit by bit and before we knew it, we were looking across the Grand Canyon at one another. Maybe that is exactly what I will do. I will get back and somehow communicate that everything will be fine. She will know it's me and she will live happily ever after. I will be that pilgrim.

====//====

"We are the last philosophers."

Jimmy looks down again at his scribbled notes.

"No-one, but no-one, dies with dignity. Fact. You can be surrounded by your family, old friends even. But, you will still die all alone."

"Now, isn't the most wonderful thing about most things the final part. The climax. The crescendo. The happy ever after. Journey's end. The. End. Of. It. Whatever IT is."

"So, why not go out on your own terms. Write your own finished symphony. Provide your own crescendo. I mean, you need to plan it, of course. There's no point running home and just putting your fuckin' head in the oven, is there? Especially if it's electric. Plan it well, my friends." Jimmy nods at the observation, giving it permission to exist. More note searching.

"Timing is important. Don't underestimate that. Now, let me see...Monday is no good, beers with the boys. Don't want to miss that. Tuesday? Library books are due back then. Wednesday?" He tails off and returns to his notebook.

"Just need summut for Wednesday now," he whispers and heads to the bathroom. The wall-sized mirror is still steamed up from Jimmy's earlier two-minute shower. He ponders briefly and then outlines letters in the steam on the mirror, finishing with a flourish of two exclamation marks.

Necessity is the mother [fucker] of invention !!

It feels like Jimmy is finally getting somewhere, even if the somewhere is only circling the drain in his own psychic civil war.

====//====

Jimmy empties the contents of what's left of his stash onto the motel room desk, moving the Good News Bible to the other side of the telephone to accommodate it. There is not much left in his chemical cache. There looks to be a small pile of white crystalline powder and two pink pills. Jimmy sighs long and loud. He pauses before licking his finger and dabbing the crystals. It disappears into Jimmy's mouth and he sucks it like a lollipop for a brief while. He repeats the process until all that remains are the pills.

"Agatha Christie, you plank! It's Agatha Christie." Jimmy glares at the daytime quiz show on the screen in the corner above the desk. He tutts and returns his attention to the matter in hand and picks up the two pills. The quizmaster concurs with Jimmy. Agatha Christie did indeed write *"Dial M for Murder"*. The pills are dispatched with the last of the vodka and the contestant shuffles back to his seat, Jimmy's abuse ringing in his hypothetical ears.

Jimmy throws the now empty tobacco tin and plastic bag into his bulging case.

"Old Mother Hubbard, went to the cupboard, to get her poor doggie a bone."

He rummages around, searching hopefully for something hidden amongst his clothes.

"When she got there, the cupboard was bare, and so the poor fucker had none."

Jimmy cackles, nostrils flared, breathing heavier and deeper than before.

"She went to the baker's, to buy him some bread."

Mumbling and fumbling, he finds what he was looking for. Taking the gun out of the suitcase, he thrusts it into his jacket pocket. Jimmy spins and darts out the room, the door closing by itself with a click behind us. Louder now.

"And when she came back, the poor dog was dead!"

And we are gone, into the car park and the late afternoon sunlight. Heading for who-knows-where.

====//====

Jimmy walks past the rear entrance to the University, two stone pillars guarding a long winding gravel drive. There are signs indicating that this is very much a tradesman's access road, but Jimmy ignores them and continues walking down the country lane. After maybe 100 metres, there is a farm entrance on the left with a loose gravel footpath adjacent to it. Jimmy follows the path over a rise in the terrain and fails to negotiate his way around a large puddle that has formed in a slight dip, soaking his wholly inadequate walking shoes.

"Shite!" I can feel his mind spinning, the pills having firmly taken hold by now. He staggers on, the pathway curving between two large hedges dissecting two of the farmer's fields. Jimmy is breathing heavily now and he squelches on further to the base of an old oak tree that invades the pathway on the right hand side. Leaning backwards into its venerable trunk, Jimmy slides down it, his jacket snagging in the tree's gnarled cortex. He reaches into his pocket and pulls out the sheet of paper. A tear slaloms down Jimmy's potted face and freefalls onto the note. I re-read the words through the brackish hue.

There is no easy way down.......

Noooo, this cannot be happening. It is all adding up. If he goes, I go. As sure as anything, I cannot survive the death of my host.

The gun rests on Jimmy's forehead. He expends his last moments mouthing the words on the note. By the time he reaches the last stanza, the gun barrel is in his mouth.

Fuck! Fuck! Fuck!

I hear the click and then another from behind. Jimmy pulls the trigger. A strangled whimper dressed in blood red. Lights out.

Whooooooosh!!

Through crimson curtains I see the silhouette. It touches Jimmy's shoulder and I am liberated. I have departed Jimmy. In the absolute nick of time. We stare at Jimmy's lifeless body, blood staining the base of the tree.

And then we run.

"Hardship often prepares an ordinary person for an extraordinary destiny." – C.S. Lewis

The nailclip moon affords just enough to light up the pathway back to camp. Nature's shadows encroach on to the track as we pass the spot where Jimmy killed himself. There is still a faint trace of red at the foot of the tree, despite the forensic team's best practice. My new 'home' is a small clearing accessed via the farmer's path. There is a two-man tent with a small awning at the entrance; a hammock nestling between two large sycamore trees; a fold-out camping chair; a tarpaulin sheet anchored by four stones covering a small pile of firewood; and a small, hand-dug fire-pit occupying the centre of clearing.

To this humble scene, add this inventory :

1 x rucksack
1 x daypack
1 x small laptop
1 x toolkit
1 x transistor radio
2 x pots
1 x mug
1 x fork
1 x spoon
1 x penknife

1 x small torch
1 x ultra-absorbent towel
1 x lighter

(Not that many) items of clothing (with nametags saying Ned)

It has been three days since I left Jimmy and I cannot help but feel slightly complicit in his suicide. Dredging up old memories and stirring my voice into the melting pot of his cranium for good measure might not have been the sole cause but I feel like I was, at least, a contributory factor in hastening his exit.

The whole host-hopping scenario is hard to reconcile. I need to instil a duty of care to my host but devising some kind of metaphysical rules of engagement won't be easy. I have had a lot to think about since Jimmy's demise. If Ned had not heard the puddle splash and the subsequent expletive, I would not be here in this slightly less hopeless position today. Call it kismet, call it a fluke, I have to make the most of this new scenario. I must learn to influence thoughts, to affect actions, to sway behaviour. And I must learn quickly, as Australia seems more than half a world away.

====//====

Luckily, the weather is fine and Ned can light a fire in quicktime. He walks down a narrow track to the stream and half fills one of his pots with water. Back in camp, the pot is placed on a flat stone protruding from the fire and is left to its calescent fate. A cardboard fruit pallet box in the awning accommodates Ned's utensils and he takes the tin mug from it. The mint bush and adjacent nettlebed behind the tent provide the free ingredients for the brew. It is not long before Ned is sat in his low-slung camping chair, bathing in the small sea of flames, drinking herbal tea and listening to a documentary about the vibrant early 70's music scene in Addis Ababa on Radio 4. Each to their own.

Night steals over the land, dissolving it in a shadowy obscurity. The stars keep watch like nosey neighbours, forever spying, constantly guarding our world from the heavens. I've always liked looking at the constellations. The stars emanate a look of permanence, displaying the thought that things last forever. But they are only acting, portraying the part of the ever-present. They flare up, cave in on themselves and burn out. But we do not see their self-harm. We are treated to the same performance, night after night. One night, the celestial backdrop will change. One night in the distant future when we are not looking. In the meantime, we gaze in wonder at the night sky, endeavour to count the countless and puzzle at why, with so many of the damn things, it is still so dark.

Ned wakes early in his tent and stretches noisily, ironing out the creases his body has inherited after sleeping on the hard forest floor. We lie there in the dawn's silence filled to the brim with noise, the blank canvas of morning adorned in the broad brushstrokes of birdsong. Ned turns on the radio and digests the echoes of yesterday's news – more turmoil in the Middle

East; flooding in China; Wall Street wrong-doings; factory clo-
sures; a prominent politician's downfall. Familiar stories from
any moment in time, stories that trouble our soul, knowing we
can never actually do anything to make them better. Maybe ignorance really is bliss.

Ned emerges from the tent into a clear, crisp morning. I
would be frozen to my Australian bones but Ned does not
seem to notice the gelid air in the clearing. He takes some left-
over stale bread from the pallet box and makes his way across
the clearing to a narrow steep path that winds its way down to
a slow-running stream. Tucked under a substantial water crow-
foot bush is a collapsible shrimp trap and Ned tears the bread
into pieces and feeds the bait into the funnelled entrance to
the net. He then submerges the trap again, wedging it between
two rocks. He stands at the water's edge, immobile, absorbing
the serenity of the scene and the mesmeric qualities of the ed-
dy's trickles. It is maybe three minutes before the stream releas-
es Ned from its lure. Three minutes lost, but not three minutes
wasted.

Ned packs his essentials into a daypack (laptop, notepad, pens),
along with a pair of shorts and a tee-shirt and secures the tent
and its contents. I know the routine now. Secure the site and
head down the path, past Jimmy's tree, to the road which leads
to the back entrance and then on to the university gym for a
quick change into the t-shirt and shorts, a 30-minute session
on the rowing machine, followed by a long, lingering shower.
Refreshed, but obviously ravenous, Ned chomps through an
out-of-date muesli bar from the bottom of his daypack, whilst

changing back into his daytime clothes. Early morning routine over, it is time for the next phase – a visit to Alec, the University porter's lodge in the grounds of the campus, for a percolated coffee and a daily chat about all things philosophical. Or what Alec calls, "banging the world to rights".

"Come in. Come in. One to do", Alec thrusts the newspaper into Ned's face as a way of greeting. It is the cryptic crossword from yesterday's paper. Amongst the slew of black ink added to the crossword grid in the bottom corner, there is a white void waiting to be filled. Ned looks at the offending clue. There are three letters already in place courtesy of the intersections with the *across* answers.

22 Down – *Enhanced means to focus on scatterbrain locus (10)*

He smiles and tosses the paper onto the kitchenette worktop. Alec, already busy making coffee, turns and speaks.

"Now then, Aristotle, answer me this. If you can't change the past, then surely you can't change the future either. It's all mapped out in front of us, isn't it?"

"Determinism versus freewill. Not doing that til next semester, Alec, sorry."

"Aww, come on, humour me. Anyway, it'll be good preparation for you."

"Thought you just said we can't change the future. No need to do any prep then" I can sense Ned smiling.

"Sometimes I wish I was born thirty years later. I would have loved to have had the opportunity to go to University, to throw myself into learning. Nobody in my class did, we all couldn't wait to get out of school, to start earning, to pay our way." Alec hands a mug of steaming coffee to Ned.

"Do you really wish that?"

Alec stares out of the lodge's only window, as the Autumn sun plays peek-a-boo through the trees.

"Nahh. I wish I would have been born thirty years earlier," he turns to face Ned and fixes him with a grin. "Then, the whole crazy thought wouldn't have even crossed my mind."

Ned sips his coffee and looks at the clock on the wall. Five past nine. He takes a seat at the breakfast bar. The lodge is so small, there is no room for a table, just a protruding oblong of formica with two stools either side of it.

"I read an article in the paper on this, Ned. The idea that circumstances determine everything. We think that we've made choices, but we didn't really. It's about who you are, who your parents are, who their parents were. It's about a gigantic chain reaction of circumstances that lead us to the now. And now." Pause......"And now. And on into the future. There's naff all we can do about it. Pretty scary, don't you think?" Alec scratches his silver beard, waiting for a response from Ned.

Ned shrugs. Inside my host, I nod. I certainly did not choose to die. There was absolutely no freewill involved from my side of the equation. Perhaps there is something to what Alec is saying. But if it is true, that our futures are already laid out in front of us, then that means that there is no way I can influence Ned. Or any of my future hosts, for that matter. I will have no influence on their decision-making, no matter how hard I try to perfect the art. Fate will out. Will I ever get back and see them again? No, I cannot second that motion. I will learn to influence, to drive their choices, to will them to the bottom corner of a land on the other side of the world. I will cajole freewill, I will.

"Binoculars". Ned pipes up.

"What's that got to do with our raging philosophical debate?"

"Nothing"

"Well?"

"Binoculars." Ned points to the newspaper and makes his way to the door. "*Enhanced means to focus* is the clue. *Scatter* is the signpost and *brain locus* is the anagram. See you tomorrow and thanks for the coffee." And with that, we are out of the lodge, threading our way through campus to Ned's first lecture of the day. Through no freewill of Ned, of course.

====//====

We wrote a will together. I remember the conversation clearly. It was after the birth of our second daughter. What's mine is yours and vice versa. And what's ours is theirs, once they turn eighteen. You know the pack drill. Maddy was very insistent. *You never know what might happen, do you?* I just shrugged and turned the volume up on our new flatscreen TV.

====//====

She enters Room 239 like a whirling dervish, her own personal tornado, dropping papers and folders onto the floor as Ned watches on agog from a safe distance, careful not to get sucked into her vortex.

"Hi, I'm Natasha," she announces.

"Ned, pleased to meet you. Need a hand with that?" Ned asks, pointing at the pile of scattered foolscap.

"No, I'm good." She carries on speaking while tidying her mess, "thanks for giving me a chance to speak to you, I was running out of ideas and then you came to me like a vision, you know those dreams you get when all you can see is one face in amongst a crowd of loads and loads of people with no faces, well that was exactly what it was like, exactly like that, yeah."

"You normally don't have to make appointments to speak to people. Not in real life."

"Yeah, but your not normal." She stops, mid paper pick up, looks at Ned and grins, "I mean you're not are you, well from what I've heard, not that it's much, I mean it's not like everyone's talking about you, you know, just that you're a bit, you know, weird."

"And it's not weird asking for an appointment with someone just to speak to them?"

"Good point, well argued. Can we start?"

"Start what?"

"Our *conversation* or whatever you want to call it."

"I thought we already had."

"Yeah, you're weird," she throws her hoard of collected papers onto the table between them. The stack collapses immediately, sheets sliding to all corners.

"OK, let's just agree that I'm weird. What do you mean running out of ideas?" Ned asks.

"When you can't think of any more, you know, ideas."

"Ideas for what?"

A light bulb seems to ignite in Natasha's head. "Oh right, I get you now, you want to know why I'm here, well I was going to tell you, but then you kinda weirded out on me and you didn't really give the chance to explain and all that."

"Well, I'm really sorry. For all that." Ned plays along as Natasha opens her binder book and locates a pen.

"Full name?"

"Excuse me?"

"Full name, please, I mean you have a full name, right?"

"Err, Ned Arthurs. You still haven't..."

"And your address? This'll be the interesting bit, am I right?"

"You still haven't said why you arranged a meeting in order to have a conversation with me."

"I haven't? Oh, well if you'd let me get a word in edgeways, I might have done," she replies innocently. I have been sucked in to the scene and I suspect that Ned's mouth is set to agape mode, like mine. She goes on, regardless.

"I am Natasha, like I've already told you, Natasha Marchbank, if you want my full name like I wanted yours, and I am a first year Media and Communications student here and I have got to write a report, no hold on, what is it I've got to do, let me find it and read the title of it, hold on..." she blurts, rifling through the stockade of A4 strewn across the table. Finding the salient sheet, she goes on.

"Here it is... 'Write a 1000-word article for an imaginary weekend newspaper supplement which showcases your interviewing skills and highlights your creative writing ideas. The subject matter must be from within the University walls and the article should be engaging and/or thought-provoking.' There, now you know why I'm here. Satisfied?"

"Absolutely. But why me?"

"Well, you've already said that you're weird for a start and there are loads of stories and stuff about you, not all bad though, don't get me wrong, but you know, I believe you to be potentially..." she points at the words on the sheet for guidance, "...engaging and/or thought-provoking."

"I prefer those two words to weird, if I'm honest."

"Then that is how I will portray you, Mr. Ned Arthurs," she smiles, enticingly, looking at us for the first time, eyes like bluebells caught in a late spring snowfall.

====//====

Natasha places her phone on the table and presses a button deliberately in order to record the interview. Instead of introducing the recording, she dives straight in with the first question.

"What is your favourite colour?"

"Crikey, it's like a Smash Hits interview."

"Answer the question, please."

"Err, righty-oh, it'll have to be blue."

"Why?"

"Do you want a philosophical answer?"

"Any old answer will do. I just ask the questions."

"My life is invariably better when the sky is blue. And I have a friend called Blue too."

"You have friends?"

"Yes. Why do you ask? Are you surprised?"

"I ask the questions, remember. Are *you* surprised that you've got friends?"

"No. Why should I be? Oh, sorry, no questions, just answers, right? Jeez, you're a tough interviewer."

Natasha smiles coyly, eyes blithely fixed on Ned. Those eyes.

"OK, forget about that line of enquiry, not going anywhere was it, how about something like, you know, what's it like, I mean really like, to be homeless?"

"I don't really see it that way. You could say that I have a studio flat in the heart of nature. I have some sort of roof over my head at night, I feel safe and I feel blessed to be exposed to the outdoors and all its residual and changing beauty."

"Ooh, fancy," Natasha feigns a posh voice. She continues her questioning.

"And what are your thoughts, Mr. Ned Arthurs, on material things, you know, stuff and all that, materialism, is it called that?"

"From a philosophical point of view, a materialist is someone who believes the world is made out of matter and a non-materialist holds the opposite view.

The inability of materialism to account for the emergence of mind within the brain and within nature, more generally, calls into question the whole explanation of reality thus far outlined by the physical and biological sciences. In the simplest terms: if consciousness is not just an extravagantly improbable chance occurrence but a natural outcome of biological evolution, then the inability to account for it within the current theoretical horizon means that biological science as we know it is fundamentally limited in its explanatory scope. So, biology, according to standard reductionistic materialism, is ultimately reducible to chemistry and physics, it follows that physics itself, the most fundamental science, is unable to provide a complete description of the natural world. What this implies, in turn, is that a more satisfactory naturalistic understanding of the world may require a major evolution – or perhaps a revolution - in the whole structure of the natural sciences: the creation of a broader paradigm that includes new explanatory constructs that can accommodate the existence of mind, rationality, consciousness, value, and meaning in the cosmos as we know it."

Natasha sits mute opposite, eyebrows raised, until she finally mutters, a little haughtily, "Stuff." She tries again, "you know, stuff that you buy, from the shops and all that, like what are your thoughts on that, you know the material world of owning stuff, like what have you got and what do you want and can you afford to get what you want?"

"Sorry, I was just playing with you. I can't help but find the big questions of life really fascinating. OK, to answer your question about 'stuff'. I don't have much material stuff."

"Why not? Are you like...poor?"

"Not especially. I only really have what I need."

"Is there like anything you really want but don't really need?" For the first time Natasha sounds genuinely interested.

"I want it to be less cold at night sometimes, but I don't really need that. I stay warm enough."

"What about TV and video games and apps and all the things that make life like fun."

"Firstly, I've got no electricity and secondly, I find fun in different ways." I see Natasha's eyebrows stand to attention again. Ned goes on, "I have a little wireless radio which keeps me company and up to date with the world at large. I've got a laptop too. I even follow a survivalist you-tuber when I get Wi-Fi in the library. I can read the newspapers here too. It's not all ice age, you know."

"OK, let me ask this question," she finds the relevant part of her scribbled script and asks, "are you old school or too cool for school?"

"Ha. Nice question. I'm definitely too school for cool. I know that. But I've never been one for labelling things or following fashions. I mean isn't that a contradiction in terms, surely by following something means it's not fashionable anymore. I prefer to spend my time thinking about life, why we're here and all that jazz."

"Jazz is definitely old school. I'll put you down as that."

"Can I ask you a question?"

"Well, it's a little bit rogue, you know against the rules, but I'll let you have one question."

"Do you think that more stuff equals more happiness?"

"Yes, I think so, I've got loads of stuff which makes my life loads easier and I mean what if my friend Stacey says that she's found something which I've gotta have, I'm not going to not take her advice so I'll buy it, and I'll be happy 'cos it's not like she's enjoying something that I'm not."

"Why can't you just enjoy what you have, instead of chasing more and more? The problem with where society is now, and we're studying consumerism at the moment, is that people end up on something called a 'hedonic treadmill,' where aspirations revolve around material goods and the next new thing, but there is no reliable link between increased consumption and personal well-being. And so the treadmill keeps turning."

"I've got a toaster that has five settings, how do you make toast?"

"I have a campfire with as many settings as I want. Anyway, your toaster is not really the problem, especially if you like toast. That's fine. It's some of the other things I find mind-blowing."

"Like what?"

"I read about this app for your smartphone called *ThumbsUp* which allows you to send a thumbs up sign to any other *ThumbsUp* user whenever the urge takes you. All I can ask is why, why, why. Haven't people got better things to do with their time? Especially when all you hear is how busy we all are and how we need to buy more stuff so we can do things quicker and to make things more convenient for us."

"When an underdog barks," Natasha says suddenly, writing the words down in her book.

"What?"

"It's the title I'm giving to the piece, you should be pleased, it could have been like, 'When a weirdo whines'......" she smiles and looks directly at us.

Ned leans back in his seat, on the one hand swimming happily in Natasha's cobalt eyes, on the other desperately trying not to dive into any cerulean trap.

====//====

The rest of the day passes in a blur of Nietzsche, Existentialism and Ethical theories. During a particularly dull session on Jean-Paul Sartre, Ned's eyes begin to glaze over and I make my move. I traverse the hippocampus looking for ways in. It certainly feels different inside Ned. Where Jimmy's space was cluttered and noxious, it is much clearer and cleaner in here. Once in, I tip-toe through Ned's maze of memories. There is not much to report. Open doorways to fond, fuzzy memories of concert halls and art galleries. Celestial sounds and ethereal visions dominate the neural landscape. Let's try something. I prod and probe at one memory, in particular. I burrow in deeper, stirring the memory. Low down, cheapseats, in-the-round, contented faces as far as the eye can see, twinsets and pearls, Sunday best. And music. And what music! There is a sinewy intensity to the violin playing and, over the course of the performance, the tension never flags, not even in the slow movements, leaving the concerto to unfold as a single dramatic arc.

I am aware of a melodious echo, a background hum matching the noise of the memory. It is Ned humming, providing the soundtrack to the lecturer's musings.

"Sartre once said that we need to experience 'death consciousness' so as to wake up ourselves as to what is really important; the authentic in our lives which is life experience, not knowledge. Death draws the final point when we as beings cease to live for ourselves and permanently become objects that exist only for the outside world."

I withdraw from the memory but the humming continues. The lecturer stops and, along with every student in the lecture theatre, strains eyes on Ned. The impromptu concert ends abruptly and the lecturer sighs and continues.

"Where was I?" he sighs. "Oh yes. Sartre believes that, as such, death emphasizes the burden of our free, individual existence."

====//====

After lectures, Ned retires to the library to work on his dissertation. He finds the quietest corner of the library to make camp, away from distractions and prying eyes. Leaving his day-pack on the desk, he first sidles over to the photocopier and takes a handful of A4 paper from the inlet chamber and then heads to the books in the section marked "*Marketing*". After choosing five books, he makes his way back to 'base camp'. From his pack he extracts a black biro, an overripe banana and an apple that has seen better days. Ruining the peace and calm of the blank page, he writes in capital letters............

ETHICS IN ADVERTISING : IDEOLOGICAL CORRE-LATES OF CONSUMER PERCEPTIONS

Ned puts the pen down, stretches and proceeds to eat the fruit before thumbing through each of the books he has chosen. He scribbles quotes and references onto one sheet, a vague roadmap of subject matter on another, all the while oblivious to anything that is going on around him in the library. Students come and go, checking in and out of our line of sight, but Ned is elsewhere. Lost in marketing-speak, somewhere on the road between KPI-Town and ROI-Ville.

I have always been of the school of thought that people do not respond to advertising per se, just to what interests them. I even used to sometimes think that the ads on the television were better and more entertaining than the TV programmes themselves. I cannot remember the last time I actually took any notice of an advertisement in a newspaper or magazine and the ads that pop up on the internet are just plain annoying. Sorry, Ned, but I reckon that your dissertation is much ado about nothing. Surely, advertising is not that important to merit the 10,000 words you will waste on it. Unless the advertisement reads "Lift wanted to Australia. Urgent. See me." Now that's what I call a good ethical piece of communication.

It is still light when Ned emerges from the library and skips down the steps and turns right down the main campus drive towards the main entrance. He usually goes back to camp via the rear gate, but tonight the routine is changed. He turns left at

the entrance and follows the road for around a kilometer until the periphery of a town announces itself. The traffic is heavy,
but moving, each car carrying a sole occupant home at the end
of another working day. Some turn into the supermarket entry road, but most continue on through the market town, on
to their scattered homes, their treasure chests of living. Ned
turns in too but skirts the busy sliding-door entrance and walks
around to the rear of the building, where there are two large
skips and any number of colour-coded wheelie-bins.

"Wotcha, Ned," the voice booms from the shadows.

"Hello, Blue, sorry I'm a bit late." Ned shuffles over to the
clear PVC strip door of the storeroom. An unremarkable figure
steps into the light to shake Ned's hand.

"You took your time." There is no anger or annoyance in
the words.

"Oh, you know, dissertations and all that."

Blue hands Ned two plastic bags full of groceries. "Sell by
yesterday, thrown out today. One grateful owner needed." I can
see fruit, vegetables and a loaf of bread in one bag. Plastic-
wrapped meats and some cheese in the other.

"Thanks, Blue, you're a good friend."

Blue shrugs. "It only gets thrown out. May as well go to a
good home. More people should be 'freegans'. You still on for
tomorrow?"

"Sure. The weather's supposed to be good. We'll get a fire
going."

"Sounds good to me", Blue delves into his supermarket
apron pocket and hands two batteries to Ned. "Here, for your
radio. In case I have to listen to you philosophizing all day
again. Got your Placepot numbers? I'll put our bets on before

I come over. I fancy a bit of Sandown action tomorrow. Should be a big pot."

Ned reels off six numbers, "6, 3, 9, 12, 4 and 1. Don't care what order. Here's my pound. And thanks again."

"Good man. I'll see you at 12 then."

"Unless I see you first", Ned replies, grabbing the bags, Blue dissolving into the storeroom shadows.

====//====

Ned wakes into dawn's cotton silence, the stream murmuring in the near distance, the birds waiting for invitations to chat amongst themselves. Emerging from the tent, the scene is breathtaking. The green giants that surround the camp have lightened their heavy coats, the reds and yellows sashaying in the gentle morning breeze. Ned makes his way down the path to the stream and hauls the shrimp trap out and lays it on the bank. There are around half a dozen freshwater crayfish wriggling inside the net, anticipating liberation, just not into the frying pan.

I could get quite used to this idyllic way of life that my host has chosen, this unique statement of growing up at one with nature. But then I become aware of the cloak of autumn's beauty, disguising the brutality of what's to come. Winter's hand hovers, an iron fist in a snow white, frozen solid glove. And then I snap out of the halcyon daydream and summon my fledgling personal journey to the fore. I need to keep on keeping on. Home, I have to get home.

====//====

Blue arrives at the camp around midday. The fire is already lit and Ned is cooking up a storm. There are freshwater prawns, riverside greens and some of the more perishable contents of last night's back door dealings. Blue has brought a rucksack full of goodies – cans of beer, a bottle of wine, packets of crisps, marshmallows and a newspaper, already open at the horse racing page. It is shaping up to be a beautiful autumn afternoon.

"When's the first race?" Ned asks with a mouth full of greenery.

"Half one. We've got plenty of time." Blue reclines in the hammock, sucking on a prawn. Ned turns the radio on. What is a rolling news channel during the morning is now a sports station, and the boys are settling in for the long haul.

"It's times like this, Ned, that there's reason in your rhyme."

"It's not a bad spot."

"Not a bad spot?!? It's luvverly jubbly. Not sure I could do this full time though. I'm more of a part-timer, I reckon."

"Oh, you'd get used to it. Anyway, think of the money I'm saving.....well, not spending. On digs and all that. When I finish, I'm not going to be anywhere near as much in debt as the rest of them."

"Not sure I would get used to it, mate. I mean, where do you shit?" Blue sits up in the hammock and pulls a face.

"I've dug a pit around the back, there." Ned points over his shoulder. "Downwind, of course."

Blue laughs, "Of course."

"And there's always the college. I seem to spend most of my time there, to be honest."

"Don't you miss the telly and all them home comforts?" Blue asks, tossing the prawn shell into the overgrowth.

"Not really. Didn't watch too much when I was a kid and I've got my radio. And I can get Wi-Fi in the library on my laptop. Don't worry, I've been dragged kicking and screaming into the 21st century, you know." Ned grins, and goes on. "Anyways, I like to be bored. I am a firm believer in cultivating boredom. It makes your life seem longer.

"Now you're talking bollocks, Ned. And you haven't even finished your first beer!"

"Alright, think of it this way. I woke up this morning pretty early with nothing much to do. I re-baited the prawn pots, stockpiled some wood and had a bit of a fossick for free grub. Chores done by 8 o'clock and you're not here for four hours.

I wrap up in the sleeping bag and lie there," pointing at the hammock where Blue is, "listening to everything that's going on around me and I start to daydream. I start to make up a new world, a world that's no bigger than this wood, with animals that are part one and part another, that talk to me. And then the trees start arguing. The elms are unhappy that the oaks grab up all the light 'cos they're all big and gnarled. So the elms form a union and demand equal rights, trying to make the oaks give them equal light. And the only way to solve the problem is to start a war and chop down some of the oaks. And then it was about time to light the fire and then you showed up."

Ned gets up from the camping chair and puts another log on the fire. Blue looks on incredulously.

"And *that* makes your life seem longer? Err, righty-o. Is that what they teach you over there, my friend?"

"I'm a daydreamer, always have been." Ned taps his temple. "Helps keep me sane."

Blue raises his eye-brows and shakes his head.

"Whatever you say, Ned, whatever you say."

According to the radio, both Ned and Blue's choice of horses in the first two races at Sandown Park have finished in the first three. The bets are still on. The boys open another can of beer each, as the radio switches from horse racing to football commentary. Blue negotiates his way out of the hammock and goes to find Ned's 'toilet pit', armed with loo roll Ned has pilfered from the University. Meanwhile, Ned starts to assemble a joint with the proceeds from Blue's "biscuit tin". This will be a markedly different kind of trip than anything I experienced with Jimmy. Thank goodness. Unless Ned's daydream world comes to life, that is.

====//====

The conversation begins to get slurred around the edges. Inhibitions are parked and the chit-chat turns earnest. Ned passes the spliff back to Blue and instigates a new debate.

"Don't you think that the achievement of bringing some-one to tears is infinitely greater than the achievement of bring-ing someone to laughter?"

Blue takes a long drag and enters the fray.

"So, I punch you in the guts and that's better than me telling a crackerjack joke?"

"No, no, no. We, as human beings, are at our finest when we explore the melancholic side of human nature. Larkin's 'Un-finished Poem', the late great Tom Waits, the ending of the 'Shawshank Redemption', there are loads of stuff that makes me cry."

"OK, I'm with you," Blue nods dramatically. "But don't you feel better when you've had a good laugh? What is it they say, laugh and the world laughs with you, cry and you cry all alone."

"Exactly. It's the alone bit that makes it so special. We laugh all the time. I have laughed at least 5 times today already, but I haven't been brought to tears once. When was the last time something made you cry?"

"Oh, I dunno. Stubbed my big toe last week. Does that count?" Blue coughs and laughs at the same time, dragon-like plumes of smoke billowing from his nostrils. He hands the joint back to Ned.

"A man brought me to tears last week," Ned rubs his eye. "Just over there it was."

"What happened?" Blue turns serious.

"Killed himself."

Blue now looks shocked. "Hardly an act of genius, Ned," he just about manages to say.

"It was his suicide note that got me. You see, we reward people who bring us to laughter, but it's easy. I can make you laugh, but I can't make you cry, can I? I am simply not good enough to do that. People who bring us to the brink of tears are geniuses, simple as."

Ha! Jimmy Vince finally realizes his true worth. Not Jimmy the mirth-maker. No, Jimmy the tear-jerker! My ex, the genius.

Blue rummages inside his rucksack.

"Ahh, suicide. The most permanent of solutions to the most temporary of problems. Marshmallow?"

I never mourned my father. There are many reasons, of course. It wasn't like he didn't give me love or affection – he was always there for me when I was small and needed him for reassurance or comfort or help with things. He gave me time, but rather like a doomed marriage, I fell out of love with him. The tipping point came across a period of about three years and I can identify the exact moment it started. It was a parent-teacher interview during my first year at high school. Miss Reynolds was my English teacher, but it was chemistry on the agenda that night. They spoke for 10 minutes and said nothing at all.

When Miss Reynolds asked, no implored, me to keep a "home life" diary in order to "get me writing more", naturally, I thought nothing of it. Even when she urged me to be "brutally honest" about my feelings and the goings-on of my parents, I surmised her motives to be purely educational. Writing freely about my daily routine and when my parents criss-crossed its mundane path seemed to invigorate Miss Reynolds in our one-on-one show-and-tell sessions. She pressed me to write even more honestly and creatively about my parents in particular. I remember a few entries word-for-word.

Friday 23rd March

Woke up listening to the dawn chorus again. My clock said 06:39. That's 3 straight days now (see Wed 21st), how do they do it? Still feeling a bit proppy so I got mum to write me a note to get out of PE. Think mum might like to write a note to get out of being with dad. Heard them arguing in the bathroom AGAIN this morning. That is their dawn chorus at the moment.

And more.

Sunday 8th April

Dad and me had a debate over lunch today. I had read somewhere that koalas had more than one mate and I said that they were silly, they should stay with the same one. Dad argued that it made perfect sense because every living thing can fall out of love and want to find love somewhere else. Mum just closed the kitchen door. I biked round to Pete's to play Atari and had some of his mum's deeee-lishus banana bread.

It would not take long for Miss Reynolds to 'persuade' my parents that it would benefit me to have a twice-weekly home tutorial with her. The fact that it was when only my father was home never once gave me cause for concern. Come to think of it, nor did the fact that a teacher would take such a personal interest in helping an already perfectly diligent and adequate student who was ranked about 7th in English in a class of twenty.

And so the affair began.

Miss Reynolds would arrive, dressed up and made up a little more than she would be on a normal schoolday. We would spend around 10 minutes looking at some text or other that "explored themes of interpersonal relationships and ethical dilemmas within the real-world". She then would slip me a piece of paper with questions relating to the text and would always say, "35 minutes, no more, no less and, remember, be creative."

My answer of "I will" was always heard in stereo, my father behind me leaning against the door frame, replying in unison.

====//====

Blue's placepot bet is over by the fourth race, but Ned is on a roll. His choice in this latest race squeezed into third place by a nose according to the chaotic and excitable radio commentary. Four races down, two to go.

"The Placepot at Newmarket last Saturday paid over two-grand," Blue is now horizontal, chuckling to himself over cloud shapes. "What would you do with two-thousand spondoolicks, Ned, my hippy mucker?"

"Put it away for a rainy day. There'll be plenty of those once I graduate. Anyway, this is today at Sandown Park. It may only be fifty quid and I haven't won it yet."

"Could be a biggy. A couple of favourites down. That's what buggered me in the last." Blue lets out a massive yawn. "Did you know that Sandown Park was very nearly a lunatic asylum? I think there was a vote and they decided to build a racecourse there instead."

"We're all lunatics, Blue. The world is our asylum." Ned leans forward in his seat, "but only the loons that can analyse their delusions can be called philosophers."

"And only punters who lose all their hard-earned can be called lunatics," Blue chirps up. "That's my kind of philosophy. And my kind of lunacy too. I'm already twenty quid down. And it's not even three o'clock yet!"

I decide to delve. I want to analyse his delusions. I want to experiment, to probe, to tease, to evoke. I want to go home.

I go looking for maverick memories, anything that throbs as I surf past. I am in, then out. Like a thief in the night. Concert halls and art galleries dominate. Sounds and pictures to stimulate the senses. I linger in one. A countryside scene showing the valley between a rocky ridge and the painter's viewpoint. The space is orchestrated by a beautiful sequence of colours working through from the soft greens and beiges of the foreground with a delicate perspective that leads almost imperceptibly to the sympathetic blues and pinks of the mountain. I hear a voice. A voice lovingly expounding the painting's virtues and a young boy's ear eagerly receiving.

The composition is framed by a tree protruding from the left and its branches across the top of the picture. It leads our eye with enormous care into the distance and creates a sense of monumentality on the picture surface itself. There is an extraordinary little red brush stroke on a roof in the bottom centre of the picture which acts as a sort of pivot, leading the eye to other warm points up the composition, set off against the dominant greens and blues of the rest of the landscape. There is something hugely coherent in this picture – it is what he called his harmony parallel to nature, which was what his artistic project was all about.

I retreat. Blue is prodding Ned's upper arm. "Are you ok?"

"Huh. Yeah. It was dad. And that Cezanne. Far out, this stuff's good."

Ned shakes his head, as if to clear it, and continues.

"Dad was tone deaf meaning he was never into music, so mum used to take me to concerts and stuff. But get this. Mum was colour-blind, so she never understood all the fuss over paintings and all that. Dad was the man for that kind of jazz. He used to drag me to art galleries and talk about paintings for ages to me. I'd sort of forgotten about that."

Blue continues to stare blankly. Ned smiles and looks at the sky through the canopy of the woods, creating his own composition and simply says, "harmony parallel to nature".

The three-thirty race at Sandown enters its final furlong. A horse named *Vincent's Ear* romps home and Ned's rainy day dreaming is over for another week.

====//====

"Saving the world is only a hobby. Most of the time I do nothing." – Edward Abbey

"Good morning. My name is Worth Matravers and I am on a crusade to save the world. Our planet is a ragged flywheel. Over-built, patched up and rusty, spinning faster and faster, it's beginning to rattle and moan as it comes apart. It desperately needs oiling and some tender, loving care. And only advertising can save it."

A murmur resonates across the audience like a Mexican wave. I can feel Ned leaning forward, mentally taking notes.

"I am here today to explain how advertising is slowly suffocating our world and I am also here to reveal how advertising is our only way out of the mess that advertising has put us in. Yes, advertising, the root of all evil is also our saviour, ladies and gentlemen. And I have a dream."

There is a palpable frisson of energy around the room now. The mixture of sophomore philosophers and third-year marketing students are intrigued. It may be a Monday morning but Mr. Worth Matravers has got his disciples wide awake and ready to follow.

"I am the founder of a new breed of advertising agency. An institution that recognizes the problems around us and one that empowers advertising as a force for good. I run *Weapons of Mass Instruction* and through the power of communication, we will make this beautiful world of ours a better place."

There is sporadic clapping and a smatter of whooping and hollering. I doubt even Billy Graham got this kind of reaction at 9.30 on a Monday morning.

"I'm going to let you into a secret. A secret so big, it will make you think again, not only about the power of advertising as a force for good, but also about how politics is changing." He clasps his hands for effect, "and how together, they *will* save the planet."

There is a tangible shift forward in the room; intent tops the agenda as ears crane to listen. Even I seem to have moved to the very fore of Ned's frontal lobe. We are sold.

"Anyone here heard of Charles Bukowski?" There's a smattering of hands raised in answer. "Good. He was a great man, you know. A great writer of truths. Anyway, he said that you begin saving the world by saving one man at a time."

A student to the left and one row in front of Ned mutters "Amen to that."

"The human race has had a massive impact on our planet. Our ingenuity, our inventiveness and our vision have modified every part of the planet. Indeed, our ingenuity, our inventiveness and our vision have resulted in every global problem we face." He paces slowly, back and forth, giving attention to everyone in the audience, never rushing his delivery. He knows how to captivate. He goes on, apace.

"We now number over 7 billion and as our numbers continue to grow, our demand for everything increases – more food, more water, more energy, more, more, more. Let me talk specifically about one of these........water. In fact, hidden water. This is water used to produce things we consume but don't think of as containing water. Cars, cotton, chicken, beef. You know it takes about 3,000 litres of water to make a burger." There's an audible gasp from the auditorium. "Yep, 3,000 litres for one burger. Suppose that's 6,000 litres for a Big Mac!"

The gasp turns to a chuckle.

"You think that's shocking? Listen to this. It takes around 4 litres of water to produce a one-litre plastic bottle of water!!" The sense of shock is audible, like tinnitus.

"Yep, you heard right. Last year, here in the UK, we bought, drank AND threw away 9 billion plastic bottles of water. Do the maths. That's 36 billion litres of water wasted. To produce bottles. For water."

Ned looks to his right. There are at least three mouths wide open.

"The human race," he pauses dramatically mid-sentence, "is in a race to extinction. We need to change our behaviour. Radically. We need to consume less. Radically less. We need companies to drive this change. We need government to change."

Matravers pauses and sips from a glass of water. Lucky it was a sip. I suspect a gulp would have been classed as excessive. He goes on, finger pointing skywards.

"But here lies the rub. As far as big, significant change is concerned, politicians are part of the problem because decisions that need to be implemented inevitably make politicians unpopular. And unpopular politicians don't last very long." There is a surety about his smile. The secret promised earlier can't be far away.

"And what about big business, you may ask? Take the world's 1,000 biggest corporations. The cost of their business activities in loss or damage to the environment is well over a trillion US dollars a year." He points a finger at the audience, waving it from side to side. "A cost which you will end up paying for in the future. And your children."

"Information, persuasion and communication. The keys to the treasure chest. Joe Public is not well informed. You are not getting the information you need to fashion change. It is not being communicated to us in a useful and persuasive way." A mobile phone vibrates on a desk towards the front.

"I am a communications evangelist. I am a master of environmental and humanitarian guerrilla warfare, where words are my weapon of choice, where advertising is the agent of change." Yes, yes, Mr Matravers, but where's the bloody secret?!?

"I have managed to secure millions of pounds from government to address certain issues that face us. Yes, those politicians that fear unpopular policy decisions that effect public behaviour have knocked at the tradesman's entrance. I get to change the way we think about and do things, then the politicians will get to say how 'they' saved the planet from kingdom come. Amen to that."

Worth Matravers beckons the enrapt audience even closer. He continues his sermon, "But there's more. Twelve of the richest and powerful people in Europe have been *persuaded*......" a broad beam erupts on his face....."have been persuaded to part with millions of altruistic Euros to set the communications agenda. Media companies have even promised me some free airtime and ad space." He pauses and takes another swig of water. Job nearly done, he turns serious and barks out, "And who dares to say that advertising is immoral and unethical?!? Thank you for listening."

A spontaneous round of applause echoes around the auditorium, some students are on their feet and Ned is smiling and shaking his head at the same time.

It's time to make my next move.

"Tell him. Tell him." It starts as a whisper. *"Shake his hand. Tell him."* Louder now. *"Go on. Tell him about how you live."* Ned stands and shuffles from his seat and into the aisle. He seems caught in the rip of a sea of approval, drawn towards the now-packed stage. There are dozens of students surrounding Worth Matravers, desperate to shake his hand, pat his back and generally pump up his ego.

"Go on. Talk to him. Tell him. Shake his hand. Go on." My pleadings continue to resonate louder inside Ned's head. He begins to mutter a response under his breath........"Yeah, share my story..." is all that is audible as he barges his way, un-Ned-like, through the knot of students surrounding Worth Matravers.

"P-P-Pleased to meet you." Their eyes meet.

The touch comes. Worth accepts Ned's outstretched hand. Thank God for the male convention of shaking hands. You see a handshake, well a good handshake anyway, demands a particularly strong command of several divergent elements of influence in a single gesture. Think of the components: a swift, elegant movement toward the waiting hand, wise use of the eyes, the considered grip strength, even the rhythm of the shake is important. All that and you have to speak, too; you have to be engaged enough to muster a question; remember a name; acknowledge some common experience while you grip, shake, and release......... but not before I make my move. My transfer.

Drifting through Ned. Slowly, then all at once. I hear Ned's voice clearer than before. I see Ned's bewildered face looking at me. Me in my new host. Ned is more handsome than I had imagined. I only ever saw a glimpse of his reflection in the stream. Handsome and well-meaning, but ultimately surplus to my requirements. My journey home continues. In a man named Worth.

====//====

To : Worth Matravers [W.M.I.]
From : Oliver Cardus OBE
Re : Company Name.......again
Date : 22nd October

My dear Worth.

As intimated in our conversation last week, there really needs to be a change of tack. For me to continue to throw money into your already swollen coffers, I expect a certain amount of indulgence on your part in order to take my (rather brilliant) ideas on board.

As you know (see previous correspondences), I find the name Weapons of Mass Instruction somewhat offensive at best and downright crass at worst. What do you take the hoi-polloi for? Now, I recognise you as an immensely creative man, Worth, and I hope that you soon see sense. Please, hear me out. It came to me last night like a divine intervention. How apt, I think you'll agree!!

3000 Saints. It's perfect, isn't it? I'm sure I don't need to educate the already educated, but just in case you don't comprehend, old boy......... In Catholicism, the only true altruistic faith I might add, there are 3000 saints. And every single one of them is designed to exemplify some kind of virtuous behaviour. It's bloody perfect! Change your company's name forthwith – a rebranding never hurt anybody.

Your opinion, as always, is greatly appreciated. Your compliance, however, is appreciated more.

Yours, in altruism. Oliver

====//====

Worth lets out a sigh, closes the email, lays his smartphone next to his unfinished coffee and continues eating his fruit toast.

"Ahh, Bardo. Dear old Cardus is stirring things up again. Shall I tell him where to stick his rebranding exercise, my little beauty?" Bardo ignores the question, preferring to stare out of the window at the London traffic below.

"Think I'll just have to stall the old bastard for a while longer, until he completely forgets about it, which shouldn't be that long anyway!" Worth laughs aloud and goes on.

"Come on Bardo, it's time to go to work," Worth says, draining the coffee and heading for the door. Bardo turns and follows behind, the tinkling of toes on stripped floorboards audible.

"That reminds me. Must get your nails clipped later," Worth turns to face Bardo, scoops her up under one arm and starts to descend the narrow stairwell leading downstairs to the WMI office.

====//====

To : Oliver Cardus OBE
From : Worth @ WMI
Re : Re:Company Name.......again
Date : 23r^d October

My dearest Oliver.

Many thanks for your latest correspondence. I thoroughly appreciate your unwavering interest in our mission at WMI and will, of course, give your suggestions my full attention. In fact, when we have our AGM (date TBA btw), your name-change demands will get an official airing. Please remember that if there is to be any room for manoeuvre in this regard, it will be wholly dependent on significant, fresh funding.

Oh, and Oliver, my dear liege, please also never lose sight of the real definition of altruism – which is to say, the maximising of good consequences for everyone **except the actor**. And we cannot possibly have anyone accusing you of utilitarianism now, can we, Oliver?

Yours in good faith,
Worth

====//====

Friday 18th June

Dad and mum argue (I think that's what all dads and mums do, don't they?). Dad and me argue (I think that's two generations with nothing in common, isn't it?). But me and mum don't *argue (I think we understand each other's hatred for dad, don't you think?). Even the dog hates dad. I often wonder whether it's a coincidence that dad rhymes with bad. And sad too. I hope that I am not a bad dad making everyone sad (everyone except Miss Reynolds).*

I think that Miss Reynolds twice-weekly visits stopped pretty soon after this entry. It didn't take long for dad to move out after this time, either. When I found out that he had moved in with Miss Reynolds, I suffered guilt and sorrow in equal measure. Not a personal sorrow, though, more of an intense sorrow for my mother and loss of something she had invested a lot of love in. The guilt, however, was all mine. I had also invested a lot of love into something - the diaries – and they continued regardless. Until the day I died.

====//====

Worth addresses the small group of work colleagues surrounding the table in the centre of the office.

"Toby, talk to me. What's new on the *Protect Our Kids* account?"

A good-looking kid with a goatee rises from his seat and walks over to a flipchart on an easel a short distance away.

"OK, before the big reveal, can I just say that if this doesn't win us an award, I'll be pretty pissed off," Toby looks about fifteen but has the demeanour of a man twice his age.

"It's got to get past the client first. Fire away, young man, fire away." Worth sits in the chair vacated by Toby.

"As we know, the vast majority of kids that are abused don't report it. In fact, the majority of that majority, we believe, don't know where or how to report it. The police is such a no-go area and loved ones are either the perpetrators or aren't really loved ones at all." I finally work out what it is on Toby's t-shirt as he struggles to turn the flipchart to the first storyboarded picture. It is a large fish riding a unicycle. He goes on.

"The majority of the majority of the majority of abused kids spend a huge amount of time on the street, rather than at home, so this is where the message has to hit home. Everybody stand up. What do you see?"

There is a scraping of chair legs and a short silence, before a girl with pink hair responds.

"A sad child and a message."

"Spot on Roxy." Toby points directly at the picture. "And do you know why you see that picture?"

"I'm sure you're about to tell me"

"Because you are an average height lady and average height ladies, as well as above average height ladies, see the same thing. What do you see Andy?"

A pony-tail in a waistcoat answers, "Sad kid. Strapline. Same."

"That is because you too, Andy, are of average or possibly above average height. And this communication solution does not discriminate by gender." Toby seems pleased with the way things are going. The rest look baffled. Another picture appears as Toby manoeuvres the sheet over the top of the easel.

"What now?"

"Abused child. Bruises on his face," both Andy and Roxy in unison this time.

"And a different message........ahh, ok."

"And do you know why you see *that* picture?" He doesn't wait for a response.

"Because you are an abused child of below average height. Which means that only children can see the message. It's a kind of secret. A bit like what they're hiding, I suppose."

"Err, clever." I'm not sure Andy is quite so impressed.

"So, inner city bus shelters. Loads of them. Anyone taller than four feet, five inches—looking at it they only see the image of a sad child and the message: *"sometimes, child abuse is only visible to the child suffering it."* But when a child looks at the ad, they see bruises on the boy's face and a different message: *"if somebody hurts you, phone us and we'll help you"* alongside the foundation's phone number. The ad is designed to empower kids, particularly if their abuser happens to be standing right next to them. It's brilliant. I found this company that can produce these lenticular boards which show different things depending on where you view them from. And the winner of the Campaign of the Year goes to.......?" Toby leaves the question hanging in the air.

"What's the bottom line in terms of media, Toby?" Worth immerses himself in the semantics.

"Reckon we can call in a couple of favours and get the whole shooting match for a couple of hundred clicks." Toby doesn't even hesitate at the question.

"I'll get Cardus to pick up the tab on this one. He's always been interested in the welfare of little boys. Nice work, Toby." Worth stands to let Toby sit down again, but the fish on a unicycle hasn't finished yet.

"Sorry Worth, can I run something else by you all? I've found another company that can do really clever things with fluorescent lights and I asked them to mock up a couple of executions for me." Toby retrieves 2 large pieces of card from his folio.

"This'll get to you," he goes on, "these ads are printed in fluorescent ink as to appear normal with a child playing or innocently laying in bed. You are invited to *"Turn off the lights and help whoever the kid is overcome his or her fear of the dark."* When you turn the lights off, a new image appears revealing a grown man doing improper things with the little kids. A new message is also shown describing the abuse: *"You might not see it, but it could be happening. 70% of child abuse cases take place in their own home."* Hard-hitting, eh?"

The room is silent. I think it is brilliant and I'm guessing by the lack of clamour in the air that the others think the same.

"Wow" Andy breaks the lull. Roxy looks like she is wiping a tear from her eye.

"*That* is what I'm talking about!" Worth stands up and approaches Toby, resting a hand on his shoulder.

"This is what the word wonder was invented for. For that moment when you're filled with admiration and awe. For that moment when you realize the beauty of what's in front of you. For that moment when we marvel. We should do more marveling, don't you think," slapping Toby firmly between the blades.

====//====

To : Worth Matravers [3000 Saints?!?]
From : Oliver Cardus OBE
Re : New campaign
Date : 24th October

Worth, old boy.

I will get straight to the point, as is often my way.

I have a great big bloody hole burning in my pocket and I cannot stand it any longer. You intimated in our last correspondence about your desire for fresh funding. The name change can wait for the moment – I want to "do" something much more worthy than that.

*You know, it came to me last night. I was looking at some words I had scribbled on a page and there it was. Words. Made up of letters. Little symbols, black on white, reducing people to tears, occasioning laughter, manipulating the world. Yes, those 26 different markings have changed, and will continue to change, the world. Whether it be the wonder of Joyce, the wit of Wodehouse or the wisdom of Ogilvy, words matter. And there are millions of children who have no access to this wondrous cave. We **must** literate the illiterate. We **must** liberate the lexicon into their lives. Saving our marvellous libraries would be a rollicking start. Why? Because everyone, and I mean **everyone**, should be allowed access to the voices of our collective past, don't you think, old bean?*

I have somewhere in the region of two-hundred-thousand of our great British pounds available for this project and I want you to start liberating these poor people forthwith.

Your opinion, in this case, is superfluous. Your actions, on the other hand, are essential.

Yours, for the time being. Oliver

====//====

To : Oliver Cardus OBE
From : Worth @ WMI
Re : Burning holes
Date : 25th October

Oliver.

    Many thanks for your latest correspondence. I must admit that I have been seldom happier to hear about a wardrobe malfunction such as a hole in your pocket! It would be an honour, not to mention expedient, to help you disburse the said monies. I will get my creative department on the case straight away. I am positive that we can make some kind of difference.

    As one of our trusted and loyal contributors, I would like you to accompany me on a business trip. I will be shooting a campaign in Amsterdam later this week and think you should be able to see firsthand the fruits of your donations. Of course, it remains to be seen if you will be tempted by any of the other kind of fruits on offer ;-))

    Let me know as soon as and I shall get Roxy to sort out your travel details.
Yours always,
Worth

====//====

To : Worth Matravers
From : Oliver Cardus OBE
Re : Amsterdam

Date : 24th October

My dear boy.

I am most gratified by your kind offer. Old Aemstrelredamme is such a wonderful place and I very much look forward to opening its treasure chest once again – it has been far too long! May I enquire of the campaign mentioned in your discourse?

I sincerely hope that we have sufficient time to visit a remarkable gin-tasting house called De Drie Fleschjes. It is one of the few proeflokalen left in the city and used to be one of my favourite haunts. Did you know that Dutch gin is very different to British gin? It is made with barley and distilled in wood, giving a stronger, smokier taste – much better than the fermented molasses peddled here!

As you can detect, I am very taken by your invitation and will pack without delay.

Yours in gratitude, Oliver

====//====

It is 9.55am and it has taken Worth almost an hour in a taxi to go approximately one mile. He sits unfussed though, a barometer of calm. When the cab finally pulls up in front of the twin pillars that guard the façade of our destination, Worth casually slides a fifty pound note through the narrow grill dissecting back from front.

"Keep the change, governor," he shouts, opening the taxi door and bursting into the bustle of Piccadilly.

Magazine front covers adorn the walls of the reception area and we take the lift to the 4th floor. "Is she expecting you?"

comes a question from a desk in the foyer. Worth smiles at the pretty woman parked behind the question and answers with another question, "we'll find out, won't we?" marching towards an office at the end of the corridor. He raps firmly on the frosted-glass door and waits for direction. A single silhouette lurks behind and beckons Worth in with a shadowy wave.

"Good morning, Mummy Matravers," Worth announces a little theatrically.

"If I've told you once, I've told you a hundred times, please call me Louise at work," the smartly-dressed lady behind the oversized desk retorts without looking up. Framed award certificates embellish the walls – a gold here, a runner-up there, I even spot a close-but-no-cigar recommendation from the judges – a veritable tabernacle of market approval. She finally looks up and fixes Worth with a loving smile.

"And what do I owe this honour? I barely get to see my favourite son...."

"Your only son, mother," Worth corrects her.

"...you're still my favourite."

"Favourite *child*?"

"Now you're pushing it. For the record, Hope is my favourite daughter and is your equal in the child stakes. Now, you obviously want something or you wouldn't be here. As I said before, you barely come and see me."

"I'm sorry. It's no excuse, but you know how busy I am." Worth steps around the desk and plants a kiss on his mother's cheek. She doesn't resist, unlike me who adopts to stay in Worth.

"Now I can say that you're my favourite child. Well, just for this moment," Mrs M whispers. Worth returns to the opposite side of the desk to face his mother again.

"What's new on the magazine front?" Worth asks.

"Oh, nothing much. But you're not here to ask me about the health and well-being of my glossy print stable, are you?"

"Very astute of you, mother. I thought I'd come for a chat about a few things."

"Poppycock! You mean to tell me that you've travelled from EC1 to WC2, that's over half an alphabet remember, to have a *chat*," Louise snorts, "you want something very specific. I know my boy."

"Could you possibly look after Bardo for a few days whilst I'm in Amsterdam?" Worth asks, before adding, "On business, of course."

"You know I will. But that's not why you're really here, is it?"

"There is something else," Worth confesses. "Do you think it at all possible, obviously it may need a word or two from the top, that one of your highest circulating magazines, or whichever you think suitable, could possibly..."

"Oh, get on with it, boy. I thought you were a master of communication," Mrs M interrupts, sounding more like a headmistress than a mother.

"Sorry. Look, can you arrange for one of your titles to publish an in-depth interview with me. A thousand words with the man who wants to save the world. Or something of that order. What do you think?" Worth tapers off, worried about the response.

"I'll think about it."

"How about throwing in some free ad space? In lieu of my interviewee fee," Worth rather coughs the last sentence. Louise takes her glasses off and rubs around her eyes gently, careful not to smudge her mascara. She smiles.

"When will you find a good woman and settle down?"

"W-w-what?" Worth blusters.

"You heard. Maybe the interviewer will ask that question."

"Saving the world comes at a personal cost, mum. I'm sure that you can appreciate that. I've no time for a full-on relationship."

"God, you sound just like your father. He once said to me that *self-actualisation, darling,* he meant his damn business, of course, *cannot be jeopardised by anything*," she says attempting a manly voice. "And he meant it. I, on the other hand, felt I still could have my cake and eat it, though."

"And did you? Did you really get the best of both worlds?"

"At least I can say I tried. And now my cake would like to involve grandchildren, or at least the promise of them."

"What about Hope? Have you had this conversation with her?"

"Oh, dear Hope. I remember once she said to me, I think she read it somewhere, that hope is the only bee that makes honey without flowers. I guess she still believes it."

"She always was an emotional pervert. Anyway, why did you call us Worth and Hope again? You can't help but aspire to your moniker, mummy."

"It was the seventies, honey. The decade of dull. Be thankful. You could have been Kevin and Tracy."

"I'd be more thankful with that interview," chips in Worth, teasing his mother.

"OK, OK, I'll see what editorial say. No promises. It may smack of nepotism."

"You'll work it out. You're the best mummy in all the world, Louise." Worth blows a kiss across the desk.

"Just don't forget about my cake."

"Maybe me or Hope will be the next layer of your cake."

"Now that would be extremely nice."

It would be emotional

"It would be emotional," Worth repeats.

"It would be for me. Your father is a different matter."

It would be for the cake too

"It would be for the cake too," again Worth mimics the voice inside.

"What are you talking about?"

The cake would be in tiers

"Err, the cake would be in tiers." The delivery is more like a question and Louise shakes her head and raises a manicured eyebrow.

"I'm beginning to worry about you, Worth. See yourself out."

Worth rises and heads towards the door.

"I'm beginning to worry about me too."

We meet in the First Class lounge at the airport. He has his back to us as we approach. Worth places his hands on Oliver

Cardus's shoulders and gives them a delicate squeeze. Cardus turns round in his seat and beams.

"Ahh, Worth my dear, dear boy. How are you?" but before any reply can be given, he continues with a "Splendid. Just splendid."

Oliver Cardus is a spindly man with slender features and quite a theatrical face. His voice is a pitch perfect cocktail of Englishness, erudition, warmth, but above all, mischief. There is a touch of the Charles Dance about him. He stands and motions for Worth to take a seat opposite him.

"You are incorrigible, Matravers, you really are. You still haven't spilled the beans about this Amsterdam jaunt." Cardus motions to the barman to bring another drink to the table.

"I apologise, Oliver, but I've been a little under the cosh these last few days. Besides, I always had you as one who loves a surprise."

"Well, I must say, I *do* like to be blutterbunged every now and then!" Cardus winks and lets out a squeal of laughter. I have a feeling that this could be quite a trip.

Worth explains the business of the trip to Cardus. It revolves around shooting a 30-second film. But this will be no ordinary commercial. It has required a great deal of organising thus far. In fact, according to Worth, it has been "the biggest fucking ball-ache of my life." It forms the cornerstone of a hard-hitting viral campaign which Worth believes will cause "some kind of seismic stir".

Sipping a gin and tonic, Worth leans forward to address Cardus.

"You know, sometimes we can't really change the realities of life, Oliver. But why the hell can't we change the eyes that see them." Cardus nods and leans in to be almost nose-to-nose. With a pursing of lips, he says, "My dear boy. You spout some pristine balderdash sometimes, you really do."

====//====

Sometimes, I go down to the lake to think. It's like a mirror but rather than observe a reflection of something, I like to try and look through it, searching for truths and maybe some future place. I look at the future of me and Maddy in the murky depths. And the girls too. Every time I go, there is a new scenario. Well, let me clarify. It's more a variation on a theme. The theme is me leaving Maddy. There is a small workman's cottage lurking under the surface, a small garden for me to tend but, more importantly, a new start. A beginning away from the inevitable end of our marriage. It is like the lake is calling me, but then I realise the image of me walking across deserts and through rainforests I envisage in the underwater expanse is just my imagination. The lake is merely a vehicle for my thoughts. My getaway vehicle. I turn around and go back to my waiting car. I go home to my life. And silently know I will do nothing about it.

====//====

Later that day, Worth and Oliver are sipping jenever in a vintage brown bar called Papeneiland. This really is old-school Amsterdam, with massive ceiling-high windows covering two of the walls allowing an almost perfect amount of natural light in. There is wood-panelling interspersed with blue and white tiles and an enormous, dusty, Delft chandelier. An ornately decorated wood-burning stove takes centre stage and the white Christmas lights strung from the high ceiling seem to have been left up from the last festive season months ago. The whole place could be scene from a Bruegel painting, especially from our table looking out on to the canal.

"I adore this place, Worth. You could say that I practically worship it. This place goes back to the Reformation and there used to be a secret tunnel from here to a clandestine Catholic church over on the north side of the canal," Oliver, tapping his nose, signals to a spot on the opposite side of the road through the window. He picks up his tulip-shaped glass and begins to hold court.

"Tomorrow, you work. Tonight, we'll have some fun. Now listen up, my pretty young thing. You will now be taught how to take your medicine. Repeat after me," Oliver widens his mouth into a kind of manic grin and exposes his teeth, "ye-NAY-ver."

He enunciates every syllable, as if teaching a two-year old to speak.

"Ye-NEE-ver," repeats Worth.

"NAY," spits Oliver.

"NAY," is Worth's instantaneous comeback.

"And again...... ye-NAY-ver."

"Ye-NAY-ver. Got it."

"Now you can pronounce the dashed thing, let me go Dutch with you, excuse the pun, on the properties of this ethereal elixir." A well-dressed older couple squeeze onto the small table next to us, making Oliver pause. Once they are seated, he goes on with the lesson.

"Yes, you heard me precisely, Worth. It is a medicine. At least, that's what they said when they began shilling it in pharmacies around here about four-hundred years ago. There are a variety of curative herbs crammed in here, number one of which is juniper. Or ye-nay-ver, as they say in these parts. It helps digestion and your waterworks. Bloody marvelous stuff, I should coco."

"I'm guessing there's a special way of tasting it," Worth interjects, "like the old Frenchies and their wine."

"There is indeed, old chum. In fact, I have my own tried-and-trusted method. Are you following?" With this, Oliver reaches for his glass and positions it under his nose.

"So far, so French," Worth is mimicking every movement.

Oliver then begins to tilt his head from side to side, like an upside-down pendulum.

"Err, righty-ho," Worth looks questioningly at Oliver, "please explain."

"Nadi Shodhan pranayama, old boy. It's a breathing technique that helps clear out blocked energy channels in the body, which in turn calms the mind. Alternate nostril breathing is just so de rigeur. So, why not do it whilst breathing in the delicious aroma of the jenever?" Oliver now seems to be in a trance, head swinging, eyes closed. He stops suddenly and lifts the glass to in front of his closed right eye. With this, he opens both of his eyes and stares at the liquid through the spectrum of glass. Worth copies and mutters.

"Cardus, what the hell am I looking for?"

"Pale, golden hues. Like a straw bale on a glorious summer's day." Oliver then lifts the glass to his ear and listens to the opening. Yes, he is actually *listening* to his drink.

"Oh, for goodness sake, Cardus, you old fool."

"It's all about the senses, my darling. You smell, you see, you hear, now you touch. Come on, keep up." Oliver now puts his index finger into the glass and then rubs the liquid onto his bottom lip.

"Can you feel it burning? Can you feel the *bite*?"

"No, what's next? Taste, I hope." Worth beats Oliver to the chase and knocks back the gin in one. Oliver looks on aghast.

"That's NOT how you taste, you heathen! You have to do the chicken's arse," Oliver protests, sucking in his cheeks and transforming his mouth into a narrow pout all at once. His eyes bulge comically. He noisily sucks in the jenever through the tapered orifice and savours the final element of the tasting journey, eyes closed.

"You are one hell of an eccentric old buffoon, Cardus."

Oliver opens his eyes again, turns to Worth and simply says, "I love you too."

I decide to go for a meander, deeper into the recesses of Worth's brain. I barely know anything about the man apart from his external confidence and desire to change things. I tried earlier today on the flight over but only skimmed the surface and was met by silence. A pitch black silence. Have you ever tried walking in the pitch black? Not a half-light or something that's just very dark. I'm talking about the blackest black you can imagine. Don't get me wrong, there are plenty of lights in here. You can cruise down his streams of thought quite happily for hours on end, but they are all stuck in the present. There must be some memories in here somewhere.

I carom down his memory canals, hoping the ricochets don't set off alarm bells in him. But there is nothing. Not here near the surface anyway. I think it is time for another experiment. I hurtle headlong into the darkness. It is time to gatecrash the party his long-term memories are holding somewhere in here. There is a fork in the cortex ahead of me, both avenues shadowy and piceous. I head left and let out a roar, hoping to wake the memories from their slumbers. The noise reverberates for a while then dissipates down the rayless corridor. I retreat.

Worth and Oliver have been sampling some of the extraordinarily named juniper-based liqueurs that adorn the shelves behind the bar. They have already partaken in some *Bride's Tears* and a *Parrott Soup*. Worth is now testing a shot of *My Aunt's Perfume*, while Oliver seems to be rather enjoying the *Shirt Lifter*. The potency of the drinks is now having an obvious effect. Discussions are in full flow.

The Big Bang Theory was actually first proposed by a catholic Priest (Oliver); the sad disappearance of the Aral Sea (Worth); London's best Members-Only clubs (Oliver); the heinous Pacific Trash Vortex (Worth); the magical term "hocus pocus" comes from the most sacred moment in Catholic ritual (Oliver); and if a man avoids red meat, it improves the sex appeal of his body odour (Oliver again). They are now sifting through the female of the species.

Oliver is interrogating Worth. My roar had briefly distracted my host earlier, his eyes darting around the room trying to find its source, whilst Oliver was droning on about 'magic' Catholic rituals.

"You keep you cards close to your chest, old fruit. I don't think I've heard you talk about a special woman. Well, apart from Bardo, of course." He lets out a raucous laugh.

"That's because there is no special woman," Worth concedes, "and yet I fall hopelessly in love every single day." He goes on, "in fact, I've been known to do it hourly!"

He points to the bar. I had noticed some furtive glances earlier, but he was quickly ambushed again by Oliver's conversational web.

"The waitress over there. She's been in my life for maybe ten minutes, and yet I've fallen for her." Worth looks at her again, relishing the chance to steal another clandestine glimpse.

"Au contraire, my chou-fleur, she's not *that* attractive," Oliver comments.

"It's the gap between her two front teeth," Worth is now staring. "I'm *gawn*. Hook, line and sinker." He pretends to faint. "I'm afraid that I find imperfections incredibly attractive. I'm a sucker for a lazy eye too. A lisp or a limp. Gold dust in a filly. And don't get me started on female facial hair."

"I say!" Oliver, for once, is almost speechless.

"In love with a stranger. And normally, the stranger the better! Flaunt those imperfections."

"So, all these hang-ups ladies have about their bodies don't mean a darned thing to you. Ha!" Oliver claps his hands, a little too loudly as half of the place turns around to see what the fuss is about. "But why no special lady in your life?"

"No real reason." Worth pauses, "Apart from being crazy busy. And I'm just not very good at relationships, I suppose." He looks down at his hands.

"Poppycock!" Oliver spits, "I always thought you and the redhead Roxanne had something going."

"No, Roxy's lovely but she's a work colleague. And she has pink hair, not red."

"Ooh, is that a so-called imperfection you love to see flaunted....?" Oliver jokes.

"Shush now, Cardus. Well what about you, you old fruit?"

"I'm a shriveled old fruit, actually. Gathering dust on the shelf, my dear boy. Celebate to the core. At my time in life, I am merely an observer. I draw the line at participation." Oliver forces a smile. There is a sense of regret etched in his face. Or maybe contrition. He goes on.

"I used to have a penchant for boys. But it was just a passing phase, as my alma mater would have said. You've heard that song, I'm a little bit country and I'm a little bit rock 'n' roll?"

Worth nods.

"Well, it could have been written about me. I'm a little bit gay and a little bit straight. I like to think of me as 'graight.'"

I feel Worth's cheeks rise as his face forms a smile. "That's hardly coming out, you buffoon."

"Precisely, dear boy, I suppose it means I've just come o."

"HA!" Again, Oliver initiates a mass staring from around the room. He goes on.

"Anyhow, I have a certain feeling of separateness from the world. As I say, I don't *participate*."

"But you certainly participate in life. I've never known anybody quite so garrulous. Don't tell me you have no joie-de-vivre." Worth protests.

Oliver looks down at his hands, cradling the last drops of his drink. He then looks directly at Worth.

"I am a member of, at last count, 14 clubs. People say that it reflects a need for me to be part of the world and to connect with it." He waves his hand lavishly and continues.

"But I have this pull, this incessant pull, which is to be apart from the world. You see, I've never really joined in. Sport, music, dancing, life. I'm hopeless at it." He tails off.

"Oh come on, Oliver, spare me the violins. You're a successful, rich, and may I say, lovely man. Chin up, we've got some Amsterdam living and some world changing to do. Drink up." Worth drains his glass and retrieves his coat from the back of his chair. Oliver sighs and again looks directly at Worth. In fact, almost through Worth. It's as though he is looking at me. Pushing his chair back, mid-stand he says simply.

"Remember dear boy, inside every person you know, there's a person you don't know....."

====//====

"It is not true that people stop pursuing dreams because they grow old, they grow old because they stop pursuing dreams."

- Gabriel Garcia Marquez

Worth and Cardus are walking back to the hotel after their gin-sodden afternoon. Worth is in a light-headed euphoria, his vision on the verge of blurry. I am just enjoying the rather glazed ride. Cardus keeps stopping and pointing at things, buildings, people, signs, anything that catches his slightly inebriated eye.

"I just adore this place, old boy. Just adooooore it," he opines. They come to a junction and Cardus becomes even more animated.

"Looook, Worth, down there. You see? My dear boy, that is the wonderful Rijksmuseum. Designed by a most brilliant man. Cuypers was his name. Did I say he was a brilliant man?"

"Yes, Oliver, you did. He wasn't a catholic by any chance?" Worth teases.

"As a matter of fact, he was! How did you know? He was practically persecuted for it too. That buffoon, William the Third, wouldn't step foot inside it and do you know why?"

"Please tell me."

"He said," Cardus attempts an aloof voice, "I will not set foot in that convent! What an arse! What?!"

Worth chuckles out loud and says, "Oh, Oliver, you are something else, a real lover of life, if I may say so."

"You're too kind, dear boy. Besides, life is too long, yet life is too short, if you get my drift." He taps his nose for effect.

"Your drift is well and truly gotten."

"I would love to live for a thousand years, but only for the curiosity of it. Alas, I'm nearing my time so I need to keep up my levels of inquisitiveness. Remember, I'm an observer."

"I'm not sure I'd want to live forever. You'd see too much bad stuff and what about the yawning eternity of boredom?"

"That's right, sweet Worth. Mortality is absolutely the intensifi....intensifi...the intensification of life."

"That's easy for you to say!" Worth blurts.

"Even the mere thought of death, of cashing in one's chips, well it just acts as one large aphrodisiac to me." They finally cross the road, laughing exuberantly.

"Who would have thought that Amsterdam would be such an aphrodisiac? Ahh, it's good to laugh," Worth asserts.

"We are doomed, dear boy, with an overriding sense of our mortality. Thank the dear Lord that evolution's great gift is laughter, where every titer or guffaw is like a little drop of exorcism." Oliver slaps Worth firmly in the middle of his back, shaking me in the process.

"Yes, we should definitely thank the Lord for evolution. Let's hear it for death!"

====//====

I am thinking about my own mortality. Locking the gate after the horse has bolted, perhaps, but I have time on my hands to study the roadmap of my curtailed life and I wonder if the terrain I covered in my nigh on forty years was much different to the majority of people. Growing old is not an incurable disease, it's just that time disallows you from doing something about it. It seems to me that the accumulation of years is in direct proportion to the erosion in the number of friends you have. In your learning years, school, college, university or work, you meet upwards of 30 people every single day. From this base number you build friendships, cultivate acquaintances, cement alliances and spark rivalries. You may even have sex with one or two, if you're lucky.

The older you get, the field narrows. You see people less often, but the number may still be quite high, double figures at least, unless you are a complete arsehole. But you leave college or the town you lived in, and the circle shrinks further, to single figures because of the tyranny of distance and maybe the effort required to maintain friendships is just a little too hard. You may not like the type of person some have become, because people change, or is it you that's changed? A crisis of discontinuity ensues, marking the official end of youth. You rally, finding new friends at the monthly book club, or on the squash court weekly, or the antenatal classes sporadically. You attempt to stay youthful by doing all the things you did with your old circle of friends, forgetting that the dynamics of the group has shifted and that squares don't fit into circles very well. The reduction of numbers mark the passing of time, and the amount of friends you had when you were young and took for granted, will never be achieved again. You may be alone, but you still have something vital. You will always have those memories of youth.

====//====

Worth is briefly back in his hotel room, changing before the evening's work assignment. I elect to investigate Worth's mind instead of photobombing him as he stares at himself naked in the bathroom mirror. I dig deep into the aphotic well and happen on a hazy scene. I can make out a car journey, sat in the back, surrounded by cases and boxes. A large gate looms in, and then out of, view. A long gravel drive meanders to reveal a huge country house. Tears shroud the view now until the car drives away, the boy stood shivering on the steps, the exhaust fume trail of the departed replacing the familiar perfumed notes of the farewell hug. The tears of being alone again.

====//====

It is twilight and we have assembled outside a typical 3-storey canalside house with four huge oblong windows on each floor. Each window has been illuminated inside from both sides with strip lighting and there is a floor-to-ceiling red velvet curtain providing a sensuous backdrop. It looks like a typical brothel. There is a constant stream of people wandering past – the location being extremely close to the real Red Light District, a short walk away. The top floor windows have been converted into a huge rectangular screen waiting to flicker into life, the remaining two floors now suddenly occupied by eight scantily-clad young women, one for each window.

There are two mobile cameramen lurking in the street, plus a static camera on the wall in the middle of the first floor. Worth gives the thumbs up sign and mouths "ACTION".

A few of the girls motion for the passing trade to move in closer. They are now fully vying for attention. People begin to stop and stare. Music now fills the street. A grimy, hardcore, industrial, dubstep beat pierces the air. This is no normal 'girls-touting-for-punters' scene. An impromptu, but perfectly choreographed dance routine breaks out. One by one the dancers gyrate and pop their bodies and then come together in unison for an on-point, bump 'n' grind, twerking extravaganza. There are wolf whistles and cat calls. Some of the passers-by join in, mimicking their dance moves. All of a sudden the thumping music stops, and so do the girls mid-step, like they are petrified in ice. Up above the windows where they stand, words appear projected on to the screen. The audience is dead silent, and the look on their faces is pure shock. There is no more delirium, no more cheering and whistling. The cameras are still rolling, capturing the reactions to the payoff.

"EVERY YEAR, THOUSANDS OF WOMAN ARE PROMISED A DANCE CAREER IN WESTERN EUROPE. SADLY, THEY END UP HERE...............LET'S STOP THE TRAFFIK!"

Only Worth is smiling. He turns to Oliver and whispers in his ear.

"Look at their faces. Job done. Five more performances. On the hour, every hour. Then it goes viral. Let's skedaddle."

====//====

Worth walks down the corridor, following, bathed in fluorescent white light, the kind that makes everyone and everything look ugly. The girl enters a room to the right, motioning Worth in behind her. The lighting in here is very different, subtle, refined even. There is a wash basin in one corner and a chair positioned in the other, but the room is dominated by a large king-size, double bed. I can feel Worth's heart pacing. They stand facing each other in what's left of the dimly-lit room.

"Hello," Worth speaks breathlessly. *Not the most impressive of chat-up lines.*

"Sit down," the girl responds, patting the edge of the bed. Worth complies.

"I'm Worth."

"And I'm worthless," she leaves the words hanging and then utters a quiet snort of a laugh.

"Oh no, I really doubt that." Worth stammers.

"What would you know about it?"

"I'm sorry." My host squirms and looks down at the faded burgundy carpet, stained with god-knows-what.

"That wasn't very nice of me," she loosens a little, "I am Martika. And I am pleased to meet you, Wurt."

She has what sounds like an Eastern European accent, but her English is fine. She takes Worth's hand and traces an outline of a heart on his palm with her cherry-red nail.

"Yes, well, err, I'm pleased to, err, meet you too." Worth seems anxious. This is obviously not a situation where he feels in control. A door bangs shut down the corridor. The whole of Worth's body jolts. *Take a deep breath, man.*

"First time, mister?" She lays her hand on his thigh. He tightens.

"Not for 'it' per se. Just, you know, 'this'. Can we talk for a bit? Please."

"The clock is, how you say, ticking." Martika looks agitated, yet concerned for Worth all at the same time. She nods, "very well, talk to me." I imagine that this can't be the first time a punter has suffered some kind of stage fright with her at the helm and her hand firmly on the tiller. Let nobody tell you that living in somebody else's body and mind is boring. Excruciatingly awkward, yes. Boring, definitely not at this moment.

This seems a good a time as any to search for memories, some clues about Worth's past and hopefully some ideas about shaping his, and our, future.

I cruise stealthily, this way and that, playing an internal game of hide-and-seek. I dart in and out of colours. What was black before is now alive with different hues and iridescence. It can only be Worth's flustered state that has brought this on. I have already affected my previous hosts in different ways by dredging up memories, good and bad. This, in turn, impinged on their behaviour. For better or for worse. Worth's memories flicker within their own palette of colours. I choose yellow. I recognize Worth's mother in younger days, business suit on, court shoes off. Late summer's early evening rays intruding through the trees, a boy and his mother bouncing in unison on a trampoline. A scene of equanimity in a young boy's eye. I disengage the way I came in.

I press on through blues and green to a purple fog. A woman dances in the violet shadows. Swaying to an invisible beat, she beckons me closer. *Closer, closer, closer,* she is mouthing to me. And then, almost in slow-motion, just as I reach her, she disappears. Only the purple haze remains, so complete her evanescence. I retreat again.

Australia. Australia. Australia. Australia.

It begins as a whisper and ends as a fully-blown shouted plea. I'm hoping this will caress his subconscious and affect his decision-making. It is not subtle, but finesse is not what is called for.

Australia. Australia. Australia. Australia.

Again. And again.

I explode back into the real world. The talking has stopped. Worth is half naked, shirt unbuttoned, trousers off, condom on, Martika lying on her back in front of him, coaxing. I feel the thump of his heart. I feel his animal deep inside, haunch to heel, on bended knee, ready to pounce. Talking over, Worth is making his move.

At her. On her. In her.

Straya. Straya. Straya. Straya.

The words reverberate around. The clarity of words smothered in the heat of fervour.

Strangle her. Strangle her. Strangle her. Strangle her.

Shit.

====//====

It comes like a sleep twitch. That first moment of infatuation, of overarching paralysis, when the idea of being in love is born.

Like a hypnic jerk, designed to stop our ancestors falling out of trees, it chaperons our feelings to the attention of a possibility, the reverie of a soulmate.

Maddy was no easy catch, though. The barriers were up then, just like now. Her cautious nature, coupled with a failed recent relationship, meant I had to persevere. They call it the thrill of the chase. It was more like April showers, one minute the sun would be out and I would be getting somewhere. The next minute the heavens would open leaving me with a rather damp ego. Nowadays, the sun barely troubles us with its presence, cowering behind the stormclouds of isolation.

====//====

Eyes open. The first cringe of morning. Worth lies and stares. A thousand yards, maybe more. He is obviously trying to comprehend what went on last night. In some respects it could be considered a huge success. After all, Martika did claim that "Mr Wurt, you made me come harder than ever before". Cutting off the oxygen levels had heightened her sensations, arousing her to the point of orgasm, before she passed out on the bed. On the other hand, if he had not stopped when he did, there may be a very different, and more tragic, tale to tell. It shook me more than a little, too. Potentially getting my host incarcerated is not on my agenda. Especially as he was acting on my perceived instructions. Still, it highlights what effect I can have. Worth texts Oliver..........

need coffee AND need to speak. not good tho

Worth gets out of the oversized bed in his undersized hotel room, rummages through his case and starts to get dressed. His phone vibrates on the bed..........

150 Herengracht. See you in 10, old boy. Yours sincerely, OC

Worth emits a snort and whispers. "Oh, thank you, you old buffoon. Thank you for your wonderful ways." Continuing to get dressed, he stares intently at each of the vintage tourism pictures hanging on the walls – *'Come to Rondvaart'*, one says, another has a girl in pigtails and clogs holding a bunch of tulips and, my favourite, from Pan American World Airways which says, *'See Amsterdam by Clipper'* with a ghostlike giant windmill looming like a lowland King Kong over a typical Amsterdam canal scene.

The arranged meeting place is a modern espresso bar and Oliver is already in situ when Worth arrives. Ordering an extra-shot cappuccino, Worth sits next to Oliver on a narrow banquette in the far corner of the bar.

"My dear boy, you look frightful," Oliver begins.

"I feel pretty frightful. Look Cardus, this stays between us, do you understand?"

"Of course, of course. Pray tell," Oliver replies conspiringly, tapping his nose.

"I don't know what came over me."

"Why? Were you blindfolded?!" Oliver lets out an apologetic laugh.

"I'm serious, Cardus, I nearly killed somebody last night."

"Oh. I see."

"I was with this.....", he pauses, "....lady. I must have got a bit carried away. I caught myself strangling her. In the middle of you-know-what. She passed out. I thought I'd killed her, Cardus."

"Where is she now?"

"She came round after a few minutes and actually *thanked* me. I thought she'd be calling the police."

"Or even worse her pimp!" Oliver fixes Worth with a wide-eyed, manic grin.

"Can you believe she actually praised me for my sexual forward-thinking? Aren't you shocked?"

"Oh, dearest. I've seen more sex than a policeman's torch. It takes more than this to shock little old moi."

"I still can't work out why I did it. It just happened. Like I was forced into it."

"Ahh, the power of sex, my dear." Oliver leans in and in a hushed tone says, "it's not the flesh we crave, but the roaring ghost within."

"No, it was more than that, like an inherent force inside me, some kind of instinct."

"I'd just forget about it if I were you, old fruit."

"Not sure I can do that."

"Why not? It's in the past now. Make it a distant memory."

Worth shakes his head. "Remembering will never be the problem. It's the forgetting that'll be difficult."

Oliver pushes his empty coffee cup into the centre of the table and sports a serious expression.

"I believe in confession with all of my flawed Catholic heart. It tells the story of ourselves, eye-to-eye with another human being, owning up to all we are. Surely it is these confessional stories that shape our lives and the more honest we are in our stories, the more freedom we will gain. Well, old sport, it's out now. You've talked about it, you've got it out." Oliver goes on, "and like a wound, once you start getting oxygen to it, it starts to heal."

"But what if something like this, something more serious, takes over me again?"

Oliver can see that Worth is wrestling with this intervention, actually my intervention, and places a hand on his shoulder.

"I suspect it was a one-off, dear boy. Please don't trouble yourself anymore with it. Now, let me tell you what I got up to last evening," Oliver gives Worth a theatrical wink and sits back down again.

"Go on, Cardus, take me away from my troubles."

" Well, I was strolling through the old Rossebuurt, looking up, of course, what with the fine architecture and the like, when I saw a beautiful little plaque which said *God is mijn Burgh*. That's God is my castle, before you ask." He goes on.

"And do you know what beautiful building houses that plaque?" He carries on, not waiting for a reply.

"It's only *the* Erotic Museum of Amsterdam! Ha! Well, of course, I wander in and pay my 5 euros and spend a wonderful hour just looking. There's an exhibition of erotic art through the ages. Fascinating. And people say we're depraved now!" Oliver lets out a trademark Cardus snort.

"And in a separate room with walls painted like a kindergarten, there's a projection of the animated *Snow White and the Seven Dwarfs*," Oliver deliberates for a second and continues in slightly hushed tones.

"But in a version which could never be shown at Euro Disney! And, wait for this, the whole show was projected next to two vending machines........one selling 7-Up and the other purveying the most unusual condoms one can imagine! Now that's what I call product placement! Outrageous! And you're worried about your minor indiscretion? If I may be so bold, it merely registers as a small prick on the pinboard of indiscretion from Amsterdam's yester eve."

I can feel Worth relax a little.

"You are a dirty old man, Cardus. But I thank you for your devilishly thoughtful words. What would I do without you?"

Oliver tilts his head and raises both hands in a 'it was nothing' kind of gesture and adds.

"Never try to take away my devils, dear boy, because you may find a couple of my angels will bugger off too."

====//====

"Could a greater miracle take place than for us to look through each other's eyes for an instant." – Henry David Thoreau

"I think it's time we got you home, don't you."

These are words that I hear, although I suspect that Worth did not. To me, they are not only the end of a conversation I have been earwigging, but also the potential next stepping stone of my journey. Worth and Oliver are firmly ensconced in non-conversation, preferring to read newspapers than engage with each other. It *has* been a full-on couple of days, it has to be said. The fact that I can hear things which evade my host's radar became news to me way back in host Ned's time. I could hear a student shouting Ned's name across the college grounds in vain. Ned didn't respond and I was left wondering what the kid was so desperate to speak to him for.

"I think it's time we got you home, don't you."

It's not the words in isolation that prick Worth's internal ears, but the context in which they were delivered. The conversation had my attention for about five minutes and it was solely down to the woman's voice. It sounded *familiar*. As Worth is sitting with his back to the couple, there is no way of knowing for sure who the voice belongs to. His eyes are my eyes. I can't see around corners. Them's the rules.

It took about a minute of 'tuning in' to recognize the Australian accent. And then about a minute more to clock its familiarity. Where do I know it from? I tell myself it doesn't matter. She is Australian. She is going home. Time to get to work again.

====//====

Memories are not neat and tidy entities. They do not come perfectly formed or to order and something that happens now can bring an event that took place twenty years ago into poignant or uncomfortable focus. Tiny, irrelevant things can reignite big, profound ones: smells, noises, views, whatever. This is what I have to work with.

====//====

"Commencing session." The tape recorder is deployed.

"As per usual, you will be fully aware of *everything* that is said." There seems to be a little too much emphasis on the word *everything*.

"Please find an incident in your life that you have a precise record of. Please regress to that time and feel that moment again. Please feel precisely that innervation as if it were happening in the present."

Well, at least they're nothing but polite.

"By dragging that precise moment into the now, we can diminish the feelings surrounding the event. The memory is then compromised and the pain diluted. Do you understand?" The monotone voice pauses, waiting for a response.

"Yes." Lorelei mutters as if in a trance.

"OK. Go to the start of the incident. Tell me what's happening.......precisely."

And so it goes on. Session after session.

"Do you have a secret that you fear will escape?"

"Do you have a secret that will shame you if it gets out?"

"Go back to that moment and smell the fear again."

"What is your ruin? I repeat, what is your Waterloo?"

Like an echo. An inquest on loop.

====//====

Let me rewind a little. Her voice seemed familiar, even before I saw her.

Turn around. Turn around.

Worth, of course, obliged in due course, according me the perfect view of that voice. That voice which immediately forged the face which, in quicktime, forged the name. Lorelei Jones. I pieced together what I could remember of her. She was a TV weathergirl, well an ex-TV weathergirl, who had disappeared from public life. One minute the Logies, the next minute radio silence. She had completely vanished. New Idea had no idea. The sands of time had made her an ex-Z-lister, a forgotten talent, where-are-they-now fodder. And I want desperately to be where she was now. And, more precisely, where she was going.

"I think it's time we got you home, don't you."

The words had echoed around Worth's subconscious head, triggering me into action. Forcing someone to physically touch another person was something I had only done once – the time Ned shook Worth's hand – but now was the time to do it again and I could not afford to mess up. Lorelei Jones was my ticket home.

It was midday at Schiphol airport. Lorelei and her male companion got up to leave, collecting personal belongings from the table they had been sitting at. I needed to act quickly before my chance was lost.

What to do? What to do? Quick. Think.

There was no point in coaxing Worth to "touch her", especially after what happened the previous night in the red light district. Time ticked by. Lorelei was now walking away. It was then that I saw the plastic bag on the floor through Worth's peripheral vision.

She's left her bag! She's left her bag!

"Excuse me. You've left your bag," Worth shouted in Lorelei's direction. She turned round, glancing at Worth, then the bag in his outstretched hand.

"Oh, that's rubbish." She pivoted and began to walk away again.

What to do? What to do? Quick. Think.

Worth was frozen, arm outstretched, waiting for guidance. Lorelei turned and waved her hand, "could you just bin it, please? I'm sorry."

Oh my God, Worth, she's famous. Surely you recognise her. Surely. Ask for her autograph. Go on. Follow her and ask. Now! Before she goes!

"Excuse me again. Errm....." Worth shuffled towards her, arm still outstretched. "I can't believe I'm saying this......but you're famous.....aren't you?" Lorelei turned and fixed Worth with a stare that stopped him in his tracks. I could sense the panic in her eyes which seemed strange at that moment in time but makes real sense now. Worth was within touching distance. I moved in for the kill.

*Take your pen from your jacket pocket. Ask for her autograph. Now, before it's too late. She's famous, remember. And pretty. Tell her that. You won't get **busted**.*

"You're very pretty. Great norx too." Worth's free hand immediately covered his mouth. "I'm sorry, I, I, I don't know........". It was then that the slap came.

Bingo! Whizzzzz! Over and out! Hometime.

It's funny but, since it happened, I have remembered that slap is an old Scottish word meaning an opening or a gap in something. It was through the slap that I entered Lorelei Jones.

====//====

So, when I heard that dad had died, I could not mourn. You should only mourn the things you have lost and not the things you simply have not got. I did not have a father. I don't think I ever did and you can't lose something you never had. Mourning him would have made me a hypocrite.

Tuesday 15th September
   Dad is no more. He died this morning. Am I sad? Possibly a little, but that is only because I wanted so, so much more from our

relationship. And I vow to be a much better dad to my children than he ever was to me. Whatever happens.

Well, whatever *did* happen. I hope that my children are still mourning me now, so at least I can say that I did my job.

====//====

Lorelei sits in the corner, looking at the creases in the wall. In a small condo, on the outskirts of an unknown town, in a country I didn't expect to be in, I continue my journey.

America. Land of the brave and the home of the free.

Yes, America. Land of Lorelei Jones and now the home of me.

The road to assumption is most often the shortest path. I had assumed her home was Australia and it was only when Lorelei and her friend arrived at Gate 23 for the plane bound for Washington DC did it strike me that the shortcut I took was the wrong one.

There are photographs pinned to every wall. Most are of everyday objects or situations. None are of Lorelei. The place looks like one of those pop-up art exhibitions, housed somewhere incongruous, more statement than high art.

There is a knock at the door and Lorelei flinches in her chair. She rises and starts towards the door.

"Hello. Who is it?" she asks, tentatively.

"It's Mel. Session time," comes the reply.

Lorelei opens the door to reveal a clean-cut, middle aged man, holding a briefcase and a cheesy smile.

"OK, baby doll, time to help you with your communication. Time to become a better person, eh?" Mel enters the room, leaving Lorelei to close the door.

"But Brian was only here yesterday. I'm not ready for another session."

"Not ready? Why wouldn't you be? Why wouldn't you want to get better as soon as possible?" Mel strides over to the table and makes room for his case on it.

"Nice photos, L. You been busy, huh?" he nods at the guilty wall and opens his case. He places a hefty file, crammed full of notes, on the table. Then, he lifts an old-fashioned tape-recording device out, finding room on the table by pushing junkmail and old newspapers onto the floor with a swipe of his spare hand.

"Today is a good day, L," the cheesy grin reappears, "today, you're going to continue to disinfect yourself. Get rid of those infestations. RID, I say." Mel emphasises the word by slamming his fist onto the table.

"You ready to start? Ready for cleaning?" His manner changes instantaneously. He is quietly serious now.

Lorelei nods and takes a seat opposite Mel.

I don't like Mel, just as I didn't like Brian yesterday, or Ethan the day before. I don't like how they speak to Lorelei. I also don't understand what the hell they are doing. I only know that they are bullies and are all wearing a badge with the label, MOMENTUM, on it.

"Commencing session." The tape recorder is deployed.

"You know the rules, L, you will be fully aware of *everything* that is said."

"Please find an incident in your life that you have a precise record of. Please regress to that time and feel that moment again. Please feel precisely that innervation as if it were happening in the present."

Same old, same old.

"By dragging that precise moment into the now, we can diminish the feelings surrounding the event. The memory is then compromised and the pain diluted. SQUASHED. Do you understand?" Mel's voice pauses, waiting for a response.

"Yes." Lorelei sighs.

"OK. Go to the start of the incident. Tell me what's happening.......precisely."

Mel picks up his pen and gets ready to take notes. The tape whirrs.

"It was the first day of school and I was really afraid. My mother told me not to worry and that I am going to have fun making new friends," Lorelei pauses, glances up at Mel, and continues, ".....and school will end really soon, she said. I said I was afraid of going to somewhere new alone and that it would seem like forever. Then, she put her arms around me and said again it will go real quick and to come home as soon as the school bell rings." Mel is frantically taking notes on his notepad. I can feel a smile develop on Lorelei's face as she goes on.

"So when the bell rang for recess.... I ran out the gate and all the way home."

Mel's face is a picture, occupying a canvas somewhere between incredulity and acrimony.

"You fuckin' drillin' me?" he splurts.

"No. Of course not." I can feel Lorelei redden.

"What in God's name are you talking about?"

"You asked me to think of a memory. So I did. I regressed and I remembered.......that."

"Well, where was the fuckin' pain in that piece of shit?"

"I'm sorry'" Lorelei sounds genuine and looks down again, avoiding Mel's ireful eyes.

I retreat into her network. Her memories are there alright, about as visible and accessible as I have experienced with any of my hosts thus far. I survey the memory scene. Ghosts of Lorelei past. But there is no sign of the first-day-at-school revelation. Not a peep. I would have thought it might linger in the foreground, in the short-term car park of remembrance, but it is not there. Come to think of it, the recollections that Lorelei gave over the previous two sessions are conspicuous by their absence too. I get the feeling that she is playing some kind of memory game with the Momentum men.

There is a card game called Remembrance, which I recall playing as a child with my parents and my brother. All of the playing cards were turned face down on the floor and 'shuffled' so that there was just a single-stack jigsaw of cards. Each player then had to turn over two cards hoping to locate a pair. The trick, obviously, was to 'remember' where each card was on the metre-square piece of floor so as to turn up a pair when it was your go. I am playing this game on the floor of Lorelei's mind. I turn over memory after memory, searching for the ones that match her chosen regressions of the last 3 days. No pairs.

"You ready for the big church Christmas fundraiser, L?" Mel seems to have calmed a little.

"I don't think so. Public events aren't really my thing, you know," Lorelei answers apologetically.

"Yeah, we know that, but you're gawna come anyhows." Mel retorts matter-of-fact-ly, with a hint of threat on the side.

"As I said, I don't do public events." There's a hint of panic in her voice now.

"And as WE said," Mel raises his tone, "you're gawna be there."

I feel Lorelei's shoulders sag.

"Unless, unless you wanna make some kinda non-partici-patory donation, of course. Capiche?"

"I get it."

"Well, you know, in lieu of you entering into a non-par-tici-pay-tory capacity, the church would appreciate some kinda donation. Maybe a bigger one this time." Mel cracks an intim-idatory smile. "I mean we don't want any of your troubles get-ting out, do we, babydoll?"

"No, of course not," Lorelei is trembling now.

"The usual international transfer method will do just nicely. Be a good girl and remember, no less than last time, L. Maybe a bit more. Or a lot more." Mel is packing up the tape machine and looks Lorelei directly in the eye.

"Hey, L," his voice is calmer now, "it's a long, slow walk towards believing everything is going to be OK. You'll get there, sweet-pea, you'll get there. Just listen to us, the Church of Momentum," he points to his badge, then places a leaflet on the table.

Mel, arms now replete with recorder and briefcase, shuffles towards the door.

"Human nature is a mystery that logic cannot e-loo-cee-date, L. Remember that. I read that somewhere." Mel is halfway out of the front door now.

"The Church of Momentum bids you farewell, L. For now, anyways. Ciao." The door closes behind Mel. We can still hear him talking. "And don't forget that donation."

Through a brume of tears, Lorelei picks up the leaflet and whispers, "The Church of Momentum : The Prison of Belief - a workable way to recover your natural, spiritual power and ability in order to change the conditions in your life. Take pride and joy in your voyage of self-discovery and self-actualisation."

Lorelei wipes away her tears, sniffs and utters simply, "It's a fucking prison, alright."

====//====

Friday 4th March

This isn't the way the story of love is supposed to go, is it?

Two people, an instant chemical attraction, leading to moments of doubt, the sharing of secrets, lots of heavy breathing ;-) you've met your soulmate, you're in love. And, don't forget, love triumphs over everything. Whatever happens afterwards. Doesn't it?

Rented a movie to try and cheer Maddy up. She cried most of the evening. I don't think Rambo II was the reason for it, though. Must remember to mow the lawn this weekend.

====//====

Lorelei sits facing the wall of photographs. Her tears have dried since Mel's visit, or 'session' as he calls it. I still don't understand what is going on. It is not long before the tears start again.

"Happy Birthday, my sweetheart." She blows an imaginary kiss at a picture of a broken bottle and I scratch my virtual head.

She diverts her gaze to a black and white image of a flat car tyre lying in the gutter.

"Oh, my, look how big you are now," Lorelei whispers. The lament continues, three photos away, this time an empty bus shelter. A fresh flow of tears begins to well and then courses down her face.

"I wish it were just the two of us together. Me and you against the world, eh, kiddo?" Lorelei wipes her eyes, smudging my view of the next image on the wall.

"I'm just here, Silla, right here on this side of the wall. You'll never be alone, my precious one. I'll always be here for you. You are the sky, the wind, the weather. Always in my heart. Silla. Always." The last words are barely audible. I make out a picture through the blurred mask of tears, the figure of a plastic baby. It seems to be hanging upside down from a washing line in the pouring rain. My thoughts are falling into place. And my world is turning upside down. I am standing well and truly in her shoes as I have been to this private hell. Never mind me, I need to help her to get back again.

You think it is who you have lost that is all alone, on the other side of that wall, as Lorelei said. But it is who is left behind, on this side of the wall, who has to be the one so frightfully alone. You then need to find a soul with whom your loneliness can reside. You need to share your solitude. And that, I now realise, was the one thing we didn't do. Mel was right. Human nature really is a mystery that logic alone cannot elucidate.

====//====

We are never taught how to grieve. There are the obvious boxes that we all have to tick and we all learn in the end, some quicker than others. Walking, talking, the correct way to hold a knife and fork, riding a bike, filling in a tax return, reverse parking, how babies are made. With death comes grief and we are left to our own devices. And just like fingerprints, everybody's dealings with grief will be unique. Maybe that is why you can't learn how to grieve so why, we should suppose, teach the unteachable.

====//====

Tuesday 16th May

I'm strategically pessimistic when it comes to love and marriage. Maddy feeds my pessimism sometimes. You're never going to have everything you want in a relationship. Let's talk about sex............she wants loyalty, trust and familiarity one day, then novelty, excitement and something new another day. I told her that you can't have both. Loyalty equals boredom. Excitement just becomes jealousy. What variety of suffering does she want. She rolled over and ignored me.

====//====

Lorelei steps foot outside her front door for the first time in nearly 5 days. It is incessantly bright and her breath catches fire, smoke billowing out of her mouth and nostrils from the intensity of the cold. It is a beautifully crisp day and Lorelei walks without purpose with a camera draped around her neck. If this was part of another story, I would tell you of how Lorelei walks through a section of town you would call functional and a little run down, with second-hand car lots proliferating the scene and garbage strewn everywhere. I would tell you about the noise, the wails of distant sirens, fire, police, ambulance, all singing in different keys to the same urgent tune. Or maybe the sweep of battered cars and bicycles that taint the outlook. Or even the obvious smell of decay coming from this withering, joyless part of town. I would even tell you that it is the garbage that catches Lorelei's photographic eye, snapping an airborne plastic bag dancing on the breeze and then seamlessly turning to capture a dog rifling through an upturned garbage bin.

But the only description this particular story deserves is that this urban backdrop is at one with Lorelei's state of mind, spiralling downwards, in urgent need of regeneration. She is at peace taking snapshots of this oppidan hallucination. It's as if she sees her own mind as a bad neighbourhood, a decaying dystopia. This reflects what I now have to exist in. Regenerating her might just lead me back home. Of course, it will be easier said than done. Above, blue sky, striped with white jet streams, teases me. All going to places that aren't here, places that would be closer to home.

====//====

"Hello, my name is Lorelei and I'm an agoraphobic."

"An agoraphobe, you *are* agoraphobic."

"Oooh, my name is Myles and I'm a pedantic."

"Pedant, I am a pedant. And you, Brooks, are a shit-stirrer"

"Only when you're talking it, my little friend."

"Don't listen to these two, honey, please carry on," a woman with a kind looking demeanour interjects. It appears that she is the gathering's facilitator.

"I, err, came here tonight as," Lorelei pauses, "as something, err, I mean someone told me that I had to help myself and try to get out of this funk."

"Hallelujah to helping yourself."

"I was told that the world was once my oyster. Now it feels like my prison." Lorelei looks down at her trembling hands. Her mouth is dry with fear, every word emanates a click, sounding more like an indigenous Kalahari tribesman than a damsel in distress.

"Go on, please."

"A, err, friend asked me to explain what things I can't do anymore and I had to tell them that it was much easier to list the things I could do. And it wouldn't take very long." Lorelei allows a nervous smile to form.

"Oh, sweetheart. Can I ask you where you're from, honey. You don't sound like you're from these parts," the kind-face lady drawls.

"I'm from Australia originally. I escaped to *these parts* a few years ago." Lorelei motions with her fingers and shifts uncomfortably in her seat.

"And why was that, honey?"

There is a lengthy pause, punctuated by one of the men to our left coughing, before Lorelei continues.

"I had my reasons."

"Care to share them with the group?"

"Not on my first visit. I'm not ready yet."

"What's that in your hand?" Kind-face lady motions towards the photograph Lorelei is holding.

"Something I brought for support, I suppose." Lorelei puts the photograph between her flattened palm and her thigh, masking it completely.

"Care to share *that* with the group, then?"

"Ooh, I lurrvve show and tell!" Myles pipes up from opposite us.

"A little compromise maybe, on your first night," little-miss-kindness interjects.

Lorelei exhales deeply and replies, "OK, but please don't laugh."

"We won't, honey, we promise. What is it?"

"I call it Poetography. It's a picture with a poem kind of attached to it. It has meaning to me. My pictures, my words, my sorry life."

I can feel Lorelei redden slightly. I hadn't seen the words on the back of the photograph until now. She goes on, more confidently now.

"Being anxious is like being scared and tired at the same time, which means I have a real fear of failure and no urge to be productive in any way. I just want to curl up and cocoon myself from the world."

"Like wanting to be alone, but not wanting to be lonely. Right?" This time it's Brooks butting in.

"Yes, that's it. So I am trying to do something that is productive," she holds the photo of the broken bottle up. "And it let's me get some..... things off my chest as well."

"Well, good for you girl. Let's hear it, honey."

Lorelei holds the picture at half arms length and the rest of the class crane and squint to see the image.

Lorelei focuses on the words written on the flipside and begins.

Vial.
Blighted on the ground.
Bleeds from my shattered heart.
Cruel cruet. Not my fault, though
Fault lines crack. Like gunshot.
Dead soldier.
Vile.

====//====

Dreams never end. No matter how hard you try, there is always the bit which goes around and around and around just before where the denouement should be. It is just like in films where the train is approaching the stricken tied-up damsel laid across the railway line and in order to heighten the suspense, the train never actually seems to get any closer until, of course, the hero steps in and saves the day.

It is just like that in Lorelei's dream now. Except there is no hero in her sky. She is hiding from a faceless someone who is chasing her down endless corridors. Camera flashes afford the backdrop. As if lightning, she seeks shelter in alcoves and in cupboards, but she keeps moving, constantly looking for a better hiding place. And, of course, I know that she will never find one in her dream. She will be in perpetuity, never reaching the resolution of the perfect sanctuary. I cannot help Lorelei find safety in her dream, bar waking her abruptly out of it. But maybe I can help her find a haven in the real world.

It was me that persuaded Lorelei to go to the session. She was reading the classifieds in the local paper, scrutinizing everything from palm reading to window cleaning. Her gaze was held by a self-help group offering company with like-minded people.

Help yourself! Help yourself! Help yourself!

The command reverberated around her head. Her eyes widened at the internal riot. I continued the bombardment.

Just do it. You can't go on like this. Help yourself!

Let's get this straight. Sometimes my verbal interventions work, but most often they do not. It seems that generic coaxing is the way forward, a kind of push in the back or a polite nudge towards a collective goal. I tried being explicit with Lorelei. I whispered my old address to her countless times; demanded she pick up a pen and write to my wife; pleaded with her to jump on the next flight to Melbourne to escape both our purgatories.

Lorelei picked up a pen from the other end of the table and circled the ad, with a visible nod. OK, so admitting to having a problem and seeking help was the first part of the solution. Momentum session man, Ethan, is the next piece in the jigsaw.

====//====

Michael, my younger brother, is different to me. If I was the master of the beautifully constructed sentence, he was always the final word. If I was the promise of a rollicking night out, he was the morning after. If I surfed the dangerous breakers of marriage, he would wipe out and get rag-dolled in his, but still come up smiling.

I was two years older than him. I lost count the number of times he said jokingly that they were the best two years of his life. And I never really knew whether there was a semblance of truth in it. That was the thing with Michael.

He was my best man. He slept with one of the bridesmaids. Thank goodness it was his wife. Well, at the time, anyway. Before he cheated on her. You see, I had issues when it came to trusting Michael. But, it always seemed that he had trouble with the burden of being trusted.

====//====

Ethan arrives at the condo a little after 11 in the morning. It seems that the Momentum boys run a strict roster – Mel, then Brian, then Ethan. Same order. Same routine. I immediately recognise Ethan as Lorelei's escort on the flight from Amsterdam.

"Commencing session." The familiar tape recorder is ready for action. Again, when asked, Lorelei comes up with a memory I have no knowledge of. She talks of being tied to a chair in the front doorway of her house for having a messy room. She explains about being left there for every passer-by to see. She declares feeling hatred, not only for her mother, but also for herself.

That didn't happen Lorelei, did it? Tell Ethan you've made it up. Go on, tell him.

Lorelei shifts nervously in her seat, processing the inner commentary. Ethan stares intently at her. He has kind eyes. Well, kinder than the other two church stooges, anyway.

That didn't happen Lorelei, did it? Tell Ethan you've made it up. Go on, tell him.

Lorelei begins to shake her head. Gently, barely perceptible, at first. Now it is a full-on, side-to-side swing of the head.

"Sorry, sir," she blurts, "that's not how it was. It didn't happen that way. Or any way at all." She peters out. Ethan continues his attentive focus on her, then reaches over and pauses the tape recorder.

"OK, I see. Now why do I have the funny feeling that this isn't the first untruth you've told me?" Ethan poses the question without malice or threat, something Mel or Brian seem incapable of. He goes on.

"And please call me Ethan." He smiles weakly and leans forward, taking Lorelei's hands in his. Lorelei hardens to his touch.

"I'm sorry."

"Don't be. I think I understand what's going on."

"You do?" Ethan remains uncomfortably close to her face.

"You have an enormous amount of guilt, right?"

"I suppose that's why I'm here."

"That's why you're so-called *remembering* things from childhood that never actually happened. A lot of anxieties are closely tied to feelings of disgust."

"They are?" Lorelei looks down at their intertwined hands.

"You see, your memories….." Ethan softens his voice, "whether they happened or not, affect the reactive side of your brain. They give you neuroses and anxieties. Like the one's you've got." He squeezes her hands tighter and goes on.

"You have to lose those memories and then the effect of those memories will be gone. Discharge the sensations of them. Do that and you will be better. I promise."

I take my chance. This has to work.

Neeeeowww! Whooaahhh!

I am now looking at Lorelei from inside Ethan. She looks dolefully pretty and I can understand why Ethan's gaze rarely wanders from her. I delve deep into his recesses. I search for ammunition, something to use as a catalyst, something to cling on to. Something. Anything.

There is a whole lot of Lorelei in here. Memories from previous sessions bob to the surface incessantly. There are some from the opening of the church of Momentum in Amsterdam too. I sense Ethan inhaling deeply, drawing in her subtle eau de toilette. It is then that I realise that her smell is a cue, a prompt for memories to ascend to front-of-mind.

Help her get out of this mess.

Ethan jerks backwards, stands up and, more critically, forsakes his grip with Lorelei's hands. Contact is broken. Gulp. Ethan looks alarmed.

"What in God's name was *that*?"

"What's the matter?" Lorelei remains in her seat opposite us.

"I don't know. Something, something just happened between us."

I can see Lorelei redden. I'm guessing that Ethan is doing the same. He continues, sensing her embarrassment.

"No, no, I'm not sure I meant it that way. And, e-e-even if I did......."

"Stop digging, you fool." Lorelei's eyes narrow into a faint smile.

"You need help." Ethan blurts.

"Oh, thanks a lot." *Well done, Ethan.*

"No, I mean, I need to help you." He points at himself, then to Lorelei, as if she were a small child needing help understanding something.

"Apparently, I need to help myself."

"Why *apparently*, Lorelei?"

"Let's say somebody told me. Yeah, let's, err, put it that way." She tails off.

"Who's been talking to you? Was it Mel? I thought you didn't go out."

"Well, maybe nobody told me. I dunno. Maybe it was just me working it out. I've got to help myself. Nobody else can do it, can they?" Now she is looking directly at me, through me.

Help her get out of this mess.

Just as abruptly as Ethan stood up, he sits down again.

"Perhaps I can help," Ethan blurts. He goes on, tentatively now, "I have an urge."

I can see Lorelei raise both eyebrows.

"An urge?" She looks quizzically at him. "So something has happened between us and you have an urge? At least I'm in safe hands, then." Lorelei cracks a smile, rendering her rather beautiful. It is now that I remember her warm, welcoming face from years before, warning of flash flooding, bush fire threats and prolonged warm fronts.

"More sessions. That's what you need, Lorelei. Let's purge the bad memories."

Nooooo!

Lorelei stiffens.

"I'm not sure the sessions are helping me *that* much."

"No, of course." Ethan scratches his head. I can hear his nails digging into the scalp.

Listen to the voices inside

"Maybe, we should just.......go out."

"Are you asking me out?"

"No, I didn't mean it that way," Ethan bellows. He continues, "I thought you going outside would help. I remember what you said at a previous session. And what Mel has told me. I'm not sure how, but I think I've just put two-and-two together."

"And exactly WHAT has Mel told you." Lorelei explodes.

Listen to the voices inside.

Ethan shakes his head.

"Oh, it's not what Mel has told me about you. No, no, no, no. It's what he's taught me about Momentum and the path to inner freedom. I really think I've cracked it. I can help you. Listen."

He sits down opposite Lorelei again and words suddenly overwhelm the room.

"Some call it gut feel, some call it heart, some call it intuition, some even call it the voice of God. I call it your inner voice, your better self, reaching out. The voice inside you." Ethan looks up to the ceiling, as if searching for inspiration, breathes deeply and continues.

"You may get an inexplicable feeling that stops you in your tracks and pulls you in a certain direction. Well, that is your inner voice speaking to you. And by listening to our inner voice, we can escape bad things. We can."

"I think my inner voice might have got me into this shit in the first place!" Lorelei shrugs.

Ethan's thoughts are racing. It's getting hot in here.

"Your inner voice doesn't resonate by accident. You strike a chord deep, deep inside and listening gives us a channel to hear the intentions of our soul. Are you with me?"

"Carry on," Lorelei says simply.

"Living a life that has no meaning means you spend a lot of time seeking to validate everything and asking for permission from other people. We are taught that when we have to make a decision in life, especially an important one, there will be somebody who will have the answer. And that someone will inevitably be smarter, more experienced, more qualified, wiser than little old you."

"Yes, I get you."

"What you need to do from now on, Lorelei, is make sure that your decisions ultimately rest in the hands of the only person qualified to make them.....YOU!" Ethan points his index finger towards Lorelei and touches her forehead between the eyes. My time.

Zooooooooom!!

I look directly back at a hyperventilating Ethan who utters finally.

"When the voice inside of you is louder than voices outside of you, you have started to master your own destiny. This is about tomorrow. And you seizing it. And how you seize it." Ethan tails off and slumps back in his seat. He looks exhausted.

"Wow, I've never seen you like that. Very masterful." Lorelei mutters in a kind of admiration.

Ethan sparks back into life, but quieter now.

"There's no limit to the amount of improvements you can make within yourself. You just need to disinfect, purge those bad things. You can regain abilities you once had.......even from a previous life, Mel tells me. There are no walls outside. That's where you need to get yourself, Lorelei. Outside is the answer." He points to the door.

"Thank you." With that, she gets up and makes her way over to the kitchen. She fills a glass with water and drains it in one go. I can almost feel the water seeping down inside her.

"I need to keep hydrated, the amount of crying I get through."

"Shit! Ending session." Ethan reaches forward and fumbles for the stop button on the recorder. Panic rising, he looks over his shoulder towards the kitchen.

"I might have to erase the record of some of today's session, Lorelei. I'm not sure it really conformed with church policy."

"Fine with me. As long as you meant what you said."

"I guess so."

"Let's hope I don't bring up those memories when Mad Mel is around."

Ethan freezes. "Mum's the word," he says conspiratorially.

Lorelei lowers her eyes and says, almost imperceptibly, "Believe me, I wish mum *was* the word."

====//====

Sunday 22nd July

How the hell can I know what's wrong when she won't tell me?! Maddy comes back from her book club and is giving me the cold shoulder over something I have either said or done (unloaded the dishwasher, tick, put the toilet seat down, tick, said I love her, tick). Still can't fathom what's up. They reckon a good partner should understand you wordlessly, which is rubbish. How can you understand without words? Please, Maddy, tell me what I've done. I beg you. All I get is sulking, that commitment to not explaining something because if I truly loved her, I would know what's wrong. Aaaarrrggghh!

====//====

Brooks is already in full flow when Lorelei arrives. The usual crowd are gathered in a rough circle and he pauses as she takes a seat and apologises, shyly.

"Sorry I'm a little late. Please carry on."

Brooks returns to his story.

"Anyways. They got me by my balls, gaup here, mooga there, syphoning the stuff outta me every which ways and I'm thinking like I gotta get out. But I can't, 'cos they got this kinda hold over me. It was suffocating, like a pillow over my face." Brooks lets out a snort. "The bastards."

"The bastards." Myles agrees, like a nerdy echo.

"I mean I'm not saying they didn't help me out or nuttin'. But there's comes a limit, when you feel you gotta take it there, man. Like when you don't even wanna leave your stoop!"

"The bastards," Myles says quietly, shaking his head.

Kind-faced lady nods and interjects.

"Did you go to the police?"

"No, maam. They got you, you see. Spiritual blackmail, I call it. You do something shameful, you ask for help, some kind of redemption, you know. Then they play with you, tease you along with spiritual guidance, then they screw you. You're stuck."

I can feel Lorelei edging closer, listening with more intent now. I can figure why. It's like she's looking in the mirror. Or listening to it, anyway.

"So, if you didn't go to the police, what did you do?" Kindface asks.

Brooks points to his gut.

"Hey, listen, don't get me wrong, the church taught me some things, including this," he reinforces the gut-pointing. He goes on, "I didn't want to go out, I was scared, you know. But, funny enough, the bastards taught me how to escape too."

"The bastards," louder from Myles this time.

"Who doesn't hate public speaking?" Brooks looks around the circle for affirmation. There are nods.

"It's up there with the worst fears. You can't breathe, you can't speak, your brain goes to horseshit and you can't remember words, never mind even speak properly. But why?"

The gathering mostly shrug in a knowing 'yes-me-too-but-why' way.

"I get nervous, but quite enjoy it actually," Myles pipes up.

"Well, let's say, Myles, you always were a bit 730," Brooks snaps. He composes himself and continues.

"It's all about how it reflects on you. You may say something wrong or offensive or unfunny or stupid. Now *that's* the real fear. Speaking in front of lots of people represents that vulnerable place where I could easily make a fool of myself and not be liked because of it."

"Is that why you came here? To overcome your fear?" Kindface again.

"It's like this, lady. You can't control what other people think of you, right? How they receive your message, how they understand or interpret your words. So, what do we, as humans, do?"

He goes on before anyone can respond.

"We hide, that's what we do. We wear a mask, we don't want to be seen, because of how we ultimately see ourselves."

"Do we all hate ourselves, Mr Brooks?" Lorelei forces her way into the conversation, taking me a little by surprise.

"I see in society a lot of people who don't actually like who they are. Hands up, come on gerrum up." Everybody raises their hand.

"I mean they like things and love other people and they look up to their Gods, worship them, you know, and all that shit. Which is fine, don't get me wrong, I don't wanna preach about religion or anything. We walk this earth as human beings and we don't have the type of respect or love or whatever you wanna call it, towards self. How we see ourselves is the problem, but what is actually in ourselves is the fuckin' answer."

"Brooks!"

"Sorry. But anyways, I wanna snuff this Mel guy for real. Dead ass. He's one of dem church guys blackmailing me. But he starts giving me kinda guidance, a way out. Thing is he don't know it."

I can feel Lorelei harden. It *has* to be the same Mel. I'm glad somebody else feels the same way about him.

"This Mel tells me a few things. That we've all got abilities, even from past lives and stuff. We need to get our gift out somehow. We all have these gifts, there's no kid or buddy out there that doesn't." He swivels and stares directly at Lorelei. She shifts uncomfortably while still looking fixedly at him. He goes on.

"Look at Lorelei there and her poems and pictures. A gift. Take it to the world, babe."

The circle all turn to face Lorelei. Still eyeballing Brooks, she says, without any elaboration.

"Bloody oath. Listen to your inner voice."

====//====

Saturday 2nd January

Secret battle is a phrase that has always struck me. Surely, everyone is fighting one. I know Maddy is. But does that then not make it secret? I wish she'd let me in. To unsecret everything. Anyway, had a BBQ today and felt like a man for the first time in ages. It's amazing what an apron and a couple of snags can do.

====//====

The meeting has finished and Lorelei is walking back through the municipal building's foyer when Brooks and Myles accost her.

"You are coming with us, little lady."

They flank Lorelei on either side and practically frogmarch her out of the building.

"Where are you taking me?" Lorelei enquires, without any note of trepidation.

"For a coffee and a chat, unless tea is more your thing. I'm a chai man, myself. I find the cardamom simply irresistible. I'm trying to master a blend at home...." "Myles! Will you give it a rest, bud," Brooks cuts him off.

"Well, I *am* sorry. I was only trying to put poor Lorelei at ease."

"Putting her to sleep, you means?!"

Myles goes into a sulk and folds his arms whilst still keeping pace. Brooks then occupies the silence and says, "Not for nuttin' but, I know that you know about the church. It was all over your face. And what you said about dat inner voice. Straight outta dat bastard Mel's songbook."

"OK, you got me." Lorelei puts her hands in the air in mock surrender. She then follows the men into what appears to be a coffee lounge bar. The place is relatively busy with the post-work crowd, but they find a table in the guts of the joint, with two vintage leather armchairs and a freshly upholstered chaise longue. Brooks has already purloined three menus and hands Lorelei one and offers her an armchair. She sinks into it with a sigh. We both read the opening gambit.

We offer outstanding, specialty coffee, craft cocktails and a commitment to being the city's 'third place'. The Greeks have their Tavernas; the French have their Cafes. DC has its **Rendezvous** *– For you. By you. So you.*

Before we can read any more, a waitress arrives.

"You decided already?" she asks bluntly, leading to frantic speed-reading of the menu.

"Ooh, a masala chai for me. Heavy on the milk and honey, please." Myles pipes up.

"I'll take the beer with spicy sangrita and lime over ice. Thank you." Brooks goes next and then nods in Lorelei's direction.

"Oh ok, err, I'll have a DC Harvest green tea, if that's ok," pointing to the menu item in case there is any doubt in the waitress' mind.

"You got it." And with that, she retreats back into the throng.

"So, little lady," Brooks turns to address Lorelei, "am I right or am I not wrong?" He has a face that certainly has been lived in and the tattoos on his bulky arms have begun to stretch and fade.

"Let's say you are 100% correct on both counts," Lorelei replies earnestly. She goes on, "I am trapped inside the world of the Church of Momentum and I'm scared."

"I am so sorry, sweetheart." Brooks says quietly, with a deal of compassion.

"We are both sorry," Myles interjects.

"I've only myself to blame. Which is where they start, I suppose."

"How did they get to you? What's your story?"

"I'd rather not."

"Aww, come on, we wanna help youse." Brooks implores.

"A bad thing happened, I ran away, right into their arms," she shrugs, "they got me by the you-know-what, and to cut a long story short, I'm now here talking to you guys."

"Jeez, you must have done something real bad, lady."

"Funny thing is, the more I think about it now, the less bad it really is. But I've told them too much. They've got me. They will just out me and I don't think I could handle that." Lorelei's vision blurs as tears well in her eyes.

"Hey, don't cry, lady. I bet that scooch, Mel, has a lot to do with this."

"Yes, he's part of the problem," Lorelei says, wiping away a solitary tear.

"If I may say so, you have a lovely voice. It's very elegant and so not from around here. Almost magical, beguiling maybe, don't you think, Brooks?" Myles gushes.

I can feel Lorelei redden slightly.

"I'll bet you dollars to doughnuts, your voice is a big part of who you are. I loved hearing you recite dat poem of yours. I cudda listened all night!" Brooks guffaws.

"Thank you, guys. Very perceptive, Mr Brooks. A big part of who I used to be. I *was* on television," Lorelei opens up. "A long time ago."

"Ooooooh, a TV star!!!" Myles sits bolt upright on the chaise-long and starts to clap camply.

"Hardly. I used to present the weather bulletin on a breakfast TV show."

"OOOOOOH, A WEATHERGIRL!! How captivating!" Myles croons.

"Fuckoutahea!" Brooks responds. "For real?"

"Well, it was about a million years ago," Lorelei ruddles a bit more. "That's enough about me, what about you Mr Brooks?"

"Aww, I ain't nuttin'. Done a few things, some bad, some good, mostly good now, although I get drawn to the bad stuff sometimes. The group helps me stay on the straight, ya knows?"

"And are you still with the church?" Lorelei probes.

"Kinda. They think I am, but I'm planning a way outta there. Big styles, lady, home run style." Brooks' eyes widen and he is grinning from ear to ear. He leans back in his chair and points at us.

"And you, my sweetheart, are coming with us."

"Oh, I'm not sure I'm ready for the outside world just yet, Mr Brooks."

"Sure you are, lady. You look pretty strong to me. Anyways, that gift a'yours needs to be delivered to the people again. Trust me."

"You're not the first person to say that to me," Lorelei retorts.

"You need to back the right horse when it comes to trust. And I'm a dead cert, trust me. Ha! There I go again with dat trust thing." He tails off, chuckling to himself.

"Do you really think I could cope on the outside?"

"Well, I for one, am looking forward to the day when I don't have to sit through another excruciating session." Myles gestures inverted commas for the word *session*. He continues. "Oh, they are sooo intrusive. I've told them things even I don't know I've done!"

"Well, what's your big plan, Mr Brooks?"

Brooks puts his finger to his lips as the waitress appears with the drinks.

"You all enjoy now," she says, depositing the order in the middle of the table, without fuss. We are left to ascertain which drink belongs to whom. All three take a sip and then Lorelei pipes up.

"So, Mr Brooks, what have you got in store?"

Beckoning us closer, he lowers his voice.

"Youze gonna love dis. As the mighty Bobby Dylan said, you don't need a weather man to know which way da wind blows." He winks. Lorelei and Myles stare blankly back at him. He goes on, unperturbed.

"You heard of the Underground Weathermen? They shook up things a little, fucking a few people off a while back and then died a death."

Lorelei shakes her head and replies, "I'm sorry, I can't say that I've heard of them."

"Anyways, they took on the man and I think you got a lotta shit wichoo too, girl, you knows, to take up their mantle. The Underground Weathermen may have died a death but let's resurrect that spirit with our own Underground Weathergirl here." Brooks chuckles to himself again.

"Oooh, the church always likes to see a good resurrection, don't they?" Myles whoops.

I smile inside. *What do they know about coming back from the dead?*

It is only then that we hear Brooks utter the words.

"Who wants to rob a bank?"

====//====

The song starts with an elongated, slightly out-of-tune, organ chord. Lorelei shouts the opening line with venom.

> *I buried my heart in a hole in the ground*
> *With the lights and the roses and the cowards down-*
> *town*

Dum – dum – dum. A loud guitar riff punctuates the verse, the bassline mirroring the same riff. An incessant driving drum beat kicks in. Lorelei is bouncing around the room, yelling the words.

> *I buried my guilt in a pit in the sand*
> *With the rust and the vultures and the trash down-*
> *town*

The song builds to a climactic chorus, an orgy of distortion and reverb. Lorelei is now screaming the lyrics. Inside her head is as hot as Hades.

When I see a man, I see a liar
When I see a man, I see a liar

There is a barely perceptible knock at the door. Lorelei turns the music off and tries to compose herself in the thunderous silence. Her breathing is still erratic as she opens the door. It is Ethan. He notices her flustered state and says coyly, "I have that effect on most women."

"Come in, come in," Lorelei gasps. Ethan steps through the threshold and stands awkwardly in the middle of the apartment.

"I didn't expect to see you today. Thought it would be Mel turning the screw."

"We're not that bad, are we?"

Lorelei doesn't answer.

"I switched shifts with him. Ever since yesterday, I can't get you out of my head. I had to see you today. You've done something to me."

I can feel Lorelei processing everything. She continues her silence.

"Please Lorelei, forgive me. I shouldn't have come."

She moves towards him and finally she speaks.

"It's ok." She takes his face in her hands and kisses him softly on the lips.

I suspect that there's a fireworks display going off in Ethan's head. In here, there's barely a damp fizzle. She's playing him. And she's about to make the next move. She looks deep into his submissive eyes, almost through him, and whispers.

"Will you be my escort to the fundraiser?"

"I was rather hoping that you would come. Mel said you were just making a donation. I was hoping to persuade you. Practically all of the church will be there. I'm so pleased."

"Can we dispense with the session today?" Lorelei asks, noticing Ethan's bulging briefcase. Her eyes drill into Ethan's, beseeching.

"Err, I'm not sure I can," Ethan is flustered.

"Just say that your tape recorder thingamajig didn't turn on."

"I might get into trouble. I'm not sure I want to......"

Lorelei interrupts, "You won't get into trouble. Remember, I'm the naughty girl in trouble." She flutters hers eyelashes, in mock innocence.

Ethan sighs, puts down the case and says, "Whatever you say."

She's playing him alright and now it's my turn to try to play her. I retreat in order to look for an appropriate memory to stir her. Lorelei's filing cabinet of thoughts is in good order today. It wasn't that long ago when it felt like an impenetrable jungle. Now, the barriers are down. It's as if she is ironing in the nude in a glass house. I can see everything. I wonder what has brought about this change. Is it my cajoling her? Or the intervention of Brooks, maybe? What about Ethan? Or has she grown used to being my host and is subconsciously letting me in now?

I skirr seamlessly down her networks, speed-reading her memories. I need to find the right type of flashback, one which will drive Lorelei forward in the grand plan. Around one particular corner, I freeze. Where once was impassable, is now navigable and the memory forms in front of me. I immerse myself in its turmoil.

Lorelei is at a photocopying machine, attempting to open the paper tray. She has a ream of paper in her hand. The tray will not budge as there is a shoe stopping it releasing open. The shoe belongs to a stocky, middle-aged man. There is anger in his eyes. He spits his threats towards Lorelei, hushed but serious, deadly serious, it's in his eyes, those eyes...............'get rid of it"..........'I'll give you the day off"........... "we can't have the whole fucking world knowing"............'do it"........'or else".........one finger drawn across his throat..........menace in those eyes............ those eyes..........those eyes. I take flight. It's not the memory I want to recur.

"Are you OK, Lorelei?" Ethan asks. "You've gone white as a sheet."

Lorelei's focus finally returns. She shakes her head, eyes as wide as they will go. "Do it or else." She echoes, pushing Ethan away.

"Whoa!" There is a look of dumbfoundment on Ethan's face. "I.....I.....I...said yes, didn't I?"

"Oh, my goodness, I'm sorry. I just remembered something. Bad times. Yeah, something real bad." She trails off and then quickly collects herself, reaching for her camera, trying to usher in a feeling of normality again.

"Let me take a picture of you, Ethan. My favourite session man." Lorelei smiles again. I am not sure Ethan is convinced.

"Will I end up on your picture line?" He points to the myriad of images hanging on the other side of the room.

Lorelei ignores the question and continues. "Let me take a snapshot of right now." She positions herself and we focus in on Ethan's face through the lens. We zoom, in and out, until she is happy with the final calibration, talking all the while.

"I have to take," she corrects herself, "actually make a picture that is consummate with my relationship to the subject matter. That's you." She extricates herself away from the camera for a second to speak directly to Ethan, then returns to the lens. "It's not just a face or an object, or even a place, it's an experience to do with that time, that moment, that evanescent, disappearing thing. One moment it's there, the next it's changed. That's why it's a snapshot. Now smile, or pose, or just be you if you want. Then I'll be ready to capture the experience."

Ethan steadies himself and poses, a hint of teeth through a false, enigmatic smile. At the same time he mutters through those same teeth, "what the hell are you talking about, you crazy fool?"

====//====

Monday 19th April

There was report on the news about a missing child. Police appealing for help, the usual stuff. Maddy just stared through the screen, somewhere between oblivious and relentlessly broken.

====//====

Brooks has called a meeting to talk tactics. There was nothing out of the ordinary about the request, it was the location which led both Myles and Lorelei to exclaim "ARE YOU FOR RE-AL?!?" in unison. Brooks assured them he was very much for real and that there was more than just a symbolic reason for his choice of venue.

Lorelei enters Washington DC's International Spy Museum and immediately sees Brooks and Myles in the foyer. Brooks is beaming and Myles is shuffling from foot to foot, looking around nervously.

"How damn cool is this place?" Brooks asks rhetorically.

"Why here, Brooks?" Lorelei wants an answer.

"Yeah, this place gives me the creeps," Myles adds.

"Dem bastards are buggin' our homes, people. We can't talk there. Anyways, I always wanted to come visit, ever since it opened. And you, little lady, need to get out more. Enough why's for ya?"

We walk from room to room, taking in the array of exhibits – the Enigma cypher machine; counterfeit currency makers; vintage spy training films; radio transmitters; even lipstick pistols. Lorelei lingers at the Mata Hari exhibit, allowing Brooks and Myles to wander ahead. She stares intently at a scrapbook cocooned in a glass case. I suspect if I retreat into her, the kiss with Ethan will be ventral in her double-crossing mind. When Lorelei finally looks up, the other two have disappeared and a flash of panic briefly engulfs as she marches to catch up. She spots them in a recess, a quiet corner of the museum with no exhibits, and hurriedly joins them.

"I thought you'd chickened out for a second there, lady," Brooks is arranging three cube seats in a huddle. It looks like he is rolling a huge dice as the final seat is manoeuvred into place. We take our positions and Brooks starts.

"OK, who still wants to rob a bank?"

"Oh my," Myles turns to Lorelei, eyes wide.

"Don't worry, kid, it's a," Brooks pauses, searching for the correct word, "it's a meta-phor-ical bank weez gonna rob."

"A metaphorical bank?" Lorelei questions.

"Yeah, I wanna rob da church."

"The bastards!" Lorelei smiles at Myles's response and then asks.

"It all sounds very tempting, but how are we going to pull it off?"

"I'll tell youz, but first you gotta go back to my childhood." Brooks goes on as Lorelei and Myles listen intently.

"My pops was a hard-working man, never did nuttin' wrong. He had three heroes," Brooks' thumb shoots up to indicate the first name.

"Hoffa." Two fingers then join the thumb in the air.

"Hefner and Henning." His hand retreats to his pocket and he goes on.

"Jimmy Hoffa was a Teamster man and did a lot of good, you know, but that rat, Bobby Kennedy, had him banged up. My pop wasn't happy about dat. A lot of people weren't."

"Hefner was a fuckoutahea clever man and my old man would swear by his show, Playboy After Dark. He used to tell me that Hefner knew more about stuff than the President!"

"And then there was Doug Henning. Now this is who me and my pop both idolized. You two heard of the Magic Land of Allakazam?" Lorelei shakes her head.

"I may have seen the re-runs when I was growing up," Myles replies.

"Well, lemme tell ya this. Doug Henning is our saviour, not Jesus Christ. He's da man."

"Card tricks aren't going to save the world, though, are they?" Myles interjects.

"Listen up. We all know magic doesn't exist, that it's merely an eee-llusion, because it is all about exploiting dem loopholes in the brain." My attention is suddenly pricked. Brooks is talking my language.

"Brain hacking" is how he describes it. It makes sense. Humans have a hardwired process of attention and awareness that is undeniably hackable. When people focus on one thing, their brains automatically suppress everything that happens around it.

Brooks explains the plan in these 'brain hacking' terms. Of course, it was never going to be a bank that was to be robbed, merely the Church of Momentum.

"Misdirection and the switch. It's simple. We create a diversion."

"Ooh, I lurve a diversion!" Myles cuts in.

"People's focus gets fucked up. Their attention is on us and when dat happens......the switch happens. Your job, little lady."

"But won't it be a little obvious that the money has gone?" Lorelei is yet to be convinced. Brooks remains patient.

"Two apples, sweetheart. Dey look the same. But one of 'em is rotten. You can't see what's on the inside, can yous?"

"Oh my," Myles whispers.

"I've seen the money box dey use. I've been to a couple of their fundraisers. Extortion rackets, more like. Anyways, we get a replica and switch empty for full," Brooks says, grinning. He goes on.

"Just to make sure, we snap a photo of the box on the night, in case they change it. There are four, count 'em, four hardware joints within 5 minutes of the church. It's late night shopping leading up to Christmas too, so no issues there. Myles goes and sources an exact copy and bingo. The heist is on."

"Then what?" Lorelei asks.

"Then we hotfoot it to the airport and get da fuck outta here!"

"Where will we go to?"

"Wherever you want, little lady. You deserve it."

"Won't they come looking for us?"

"Don't worry, it'll come clear soon. We'll be a-ok, I promise. Dat's another reason why we're here." Brooks indicates towards a poster attached to a door behind us. "We pick up some tips from the top."

Great Escapes or How Spies, Hostages & Assets Survive & Get Out Alive – A Spy Seminar in Escape & Survival – 6.30pm prompt

"But they'll still come looking for us, Brooks."

"Oh yeah, 'scuse me officer, Curly, Larry and Moe made off with our money. Boo fuckin' hoo!"

"Excuse my ignorance, but who are Curly, Barry and what-shisname?"

I'm still not sure Lorelei is convinced. I'm thinking it just might be my ticket home.

"Come on drink up, Moe's gotta go."

====//====

We talk. Well, Michael talks. To be honest, there is much more to say about his life. He sees and does far more than I ever can hope to. His love life, actually his life full stop, is sufficiently chaotic and charged and replete with narratives ingrained with mind-bending, time-consuming and mouth-wide-open twists and turns in them. I am just grateful he asks me how me, Maddy and the girls are. Even acknowledging our existence feels like some kind of miracle. Keeping up with Michael is no easy feat.

====//====

I now know the plan. If it all works, we will be flying out of Washington tomorrow. If it fails, well, who knows? Let's say, probable incarceration and a huge setback in my dream of getting home.

We are at Myles's place, a small condo half a dozen blocks away from Lorelei's. I am not sure whether Brooks is late or us early, but Lorelei engages Myles in conversation whilst he flits around his kitchen area.

"I know absolutely nothing about you. How did you get to here?" Lorelei asks.

Myles seems taken aback by the question.

"Ooh, you know, nothing to tell really."

"I don't want your deepest darkest secrets. Just a little bit of who you are and how you ended up in the church."

Myles stops in his tracks and lets out the most dramatic of sighs.

"Just so you know that this isn't easy for me," he says as a preface of what is to come.

"I understand that it's hard talking about yourself. I really do."

"It's only because I don't really know how I got to here, myself. I can tell you the facts, though."

"OK, what are the facts?"

"I was born in Eau Claire, Wisconsin, and moved to New York City when my parents separated when I was thirteen. I lived with my mom, who was an event planner for a large PR company. I loved my mom." Myles breaks off for a moment, emotion rising in his tiny frame. He smiles and continues.

"I loved my mom. She would organize anything and everything. Sausage sizzles, record launches, meet 'n' greets, ambassador days, brand parties, fashion shows...oh, it was soo exciting. She knew every nook and cranny of Manhattan, every palace and every dive bar. She used to take me along to help. She was amazing. Good times," Myles tails off. Lorelei fills the gap with tenderness.

"There's a big but, isn't there? You said you *loved* your mother. What happened?"

"I had just turned eighteen when she was diagnosed. She died on my nineteenth birthday."

"I'm so sorry, Myles." Lorelei rests her hand on his cheek. I resist the urge to depart. "What happened next?"

"It's fine. It was nearly ten years ago. Well, the PR company let me intern for them for a while but I was a disaster."

"Why?"

"Social anxiety mainly. I am what my ex-shrink called an extroverted introvert. It used to rear its ugly head before the event or whenever I was expected to be 'on' for a crowd. It was draining."

"Are you better now?"

"I know how to handle it now, but mainly I don't bother putting myself in those situations. Silly, isn't it?"

"And the church?"

"That's the hardest part of the story. Oh my." He swallows hard. Now he looks visibly scared. "I think you should sit down."

====//====

Tuesday 14th March
Surely, faith is alive and well in most people who do it tough. Maddy is doing it tough right now. I hope she finds solace by doing

something. It's not struggle that kills faith, it's the inertia in your life.

====//====

Lorelei perches on a wooden chair, chisel marks up all its legs. Myles sits adjacent on the two-seat soft-bellied sofa. He turns towards us to continue his autobiography and speaks gingerly.

"When we moved to New York when I was thirteen, my uncle, my dad's brother used to come around a lot. You know, to help out my mom," Myles states, biting his lip in the process. "It started off with him showing me his, you know, doodle." Myles reddens immediately. "And it got to him playing around with me."

"Oh, poor you." Lorelei reaches out to touch Myles.

"It carried on for a year or two."

"And you didn't tell your mother? Or just couldn't, I suppose?"

"I felt guilty as you're supposed to feel horror or shock or something," Myles replies, "but I got pleasure out of what was happening to me."

Lorelei pulls her outstretched hand back.

"And then that made me feel even more guilty 'cos I thought there was something wrong with me." Myles averts his gaze and looks at the floor. He goes on.

"Like I was different to the other kids."

"Oh, Myles."

"And then when mom passed I spiralled a bit and my anxieties got on top of me. I had no real friends and I started to go online and look at, oh God, you know, pictures of kids."

"Myles!" Lorelei gasps.

"N-n-nothing that bad, I promise," he stammers. "Not real abuse. Just pictures. Underwear, swimming pool, beach, that kind of stuff. Oh my."

"Why, Myles, why?"

"I suppose when I look, I mean looked, at children in that situation, I don't feel like the adult looking. I'm not the abuser. I'm the child being taken advantage of. It's not the image or the abuse which stimulates me, it's the memories of the pleasure I felt."

Lorelei is stunned. There is a lot to take in and sparks fly inside her head. It's like a furnace in here, spot fires starting all over the place. All she can say, "Wow." She gets up and embraces Myles. I decide against entering Myles. It may be uncomfortable where I am at the moment, but his head is full of memories I really don't want to see.

"You ok?" she whispers in his ear. Sighing, Myles gently pushes her away.

"From sweet to sour, heh? There's more, I'm afraid. There was a group I joined online and they wouldn't share their stuff unless I shared some pictures of my own."

"Oh, Jesus." Lorelei and I gasp in unison.

"So, I used to go out on the subway, you know, walk around town and upskirt."

"And what?"

"Upskirt. You know take pictures up girl's skirts. I had a remote camera attached to my shoe. I would then upload them and share, just so I could get to see their pictures." He looks directly at us and says grimly, "I only really wanted acceptance." The revelation hangs, thick in the air.

Lorelei shakes her head, gravely. "Please don't tell me there's more."

"Then one of the group got arrested and I panicked. The church gave me a way out."

"They know about this?"

"Yes, those sessions can be brooo-tal," Myles embellishes.

"Who can be brutal?" booms a voice from the opening door. It is Brooks, finally, struggling with a huge video camera.

"Shit, you scared me," squeals Myles, practically jumping out of his skin.

I retreat for a second or two to find a cooler place. All Lorelei's lobes are blazing. I think this is what people mean when they say it's too much to take in. I find a space that feels less torrid and re-enter the fray. Brooks is struggling with a snake-pit of wires over the other side of the room. He waves his hand in our direction and says, "Attaboy, it's hard to let things out when you're so used to keeping the lot in. She's one of us now. I'll be set up soon. Carry on, carry on."

"Where were we?" Myles asks.

"The sessions?"

"Oh yes. The church offered me the carrot of finding some meaning in life, to improve myself and how I feel about myself. You know, to scrub myself clean and start again."

"And now you want out?"

"It was all bullshit," he covers his mouth with his free hand, "oh my, pardon me in front of a lady. Yes, I worked it out a while ago but was too scared to do anything about it. And then I met Brooks at a fundraiser and he feels the same way."

"What exactly did you work out?"

"That we are nuttin, absol-ooo-tely nuttin'" Brooks interjects.

"No, you're not!" Lorelei retorts. Myles looks as calm as I have seen him and continues.

"Oh, sweet Lorelei, we are *all* nothing in the grand, grand scheme of things. Insignificant specks in a wholly significant universe. So, I decided, with Brooks's help, to change the way I looked at my life. Simple, really. It's not like everything has to have some kind of meaning apportioned to it, is it? I don't have to change the whole world, just maybe a few other people's worlds. I have an opportunity to invent my own meaning and ascribe value to my life. And to each other as a result. I mean you wouldn't normally see someone like me spend time with someone like Brooks now, would you?" Myles lets out a camp laugh and says, "Oh my! I can't believe I just said that!"

Brooks lets out a huge guffaw. "The Three Stooges take da world!"

"Let's just rewind here for one second," Lorelei cuts in. "Wouldn't the church give your name to the authorities if you left?"

"No doubt 'bout it," Brooks ditches his wire untangling job and joins Myles on the sofa. He goes on, "and the authorities can release your name because it is not attached to a particular child that has been abused."

"You go on a register, everyone can see your name."

"But that's terrible," Lorelei protests.

"Brooks has got it sorted."

"I know some people who know some people. Myles here," he squeezes his arm, "is a proper new person. New ID, new welfare card, new everything. He starts again, for real." Brooks reaches into his pocket, pulls out a wallet full of cards and throws them onto Myles's lap.

"Oh my!"

"Am I allowed to know his new name?" Lorelei asks as Myles rifles through the wallet.

"Sure, we're all in it together. Tell her Myles. I chose it specially for him."

"I am, wait for it, can I have a drumroll, please." Brooks obliges on the arm of the sofa. Myles shows Lorelei one of the cards, "I am Richard Kimble, ta-daahh."

"Err, who is Richard Kimble?"

"You gotta lot to learn about culture, little lady. He was da fugitive from the TV when I was growing up. I kinda think it suits our Myles here." Brooks explains as Myles continues to beam next to him.

"Now, my dear Lorelei," Brooks wheezes as he tries to get up, "have you learned your lines?"

"I hope so."

"Then let's get this goddamn show on the road."

====//====

Thursday 9th May

Think I'm working it out. I watched Maddy over dinner. You never really get over grief. You just become a person that absorbs it within you. You change as a person, you don't get over it. It just becomes a part of you. The grief fills the hole. Yeah, that's it. It's always inside, no matter what. Am I any different?

====//====

Brooks wants to leave a calling card from the three of them, well Lorelei, in particular. After all, as Brooks keeps telling us, she is "the Underground Weathergirl and all."

"You deliver it in dat beautiful voice you got. For real." Brooks is directing the whole scene. "Dem bastards!"

"Ready to roll. Lights and action," Myles yelps from behind the camera.

"Make sure you hold it still. No camera shake. Or I'll shake you, my little friend!" Brooks barks and I finally work it out. His voice has been bugging me ever since Lorelei's inaugural self-help session. Brooks sounds exactly like the big dog (was it Butch?) from the Tom and Jerry cartoons.

Lorelei shifts nervously and suddenly the old routine comes flooding back. No autocue is needed as the words come straight from her heart.

"Good evening. The low depression will spread from the west, right into the heart of the city.

Generally, it will remain unsettled and a period of dense fog will persist.

Heavy rain, actually steer rods from the heavens, will drench you and even an umbrella won't shield you from the deluge.

Eventually, it will become clear.

Expect two to three feet of drama this evening with a high probability of vengeance blowing in from all directions.

Tomorrow will see a bright start and will remain settled........ for ever and ever.

It will be as hot as hell for Momentum in the coming days. Oh, and by the way, expect Satan to call wanting his weather back.

This has been the Underground Weathergirl with your weather forecast. Good night."

"And CUT!" Brooks booms from left of camera.

"Oooh, I hope that take works. You're such a pro, Lorelei," Myles gushes, looking up from the viewfinder.

"Well, you two can check it. I'm not sure I'm ready to see my comeback just yet." Lorelei retreats as the tape is rewound and checked. She grabs a pen and begins to write on a scrap of discarded paper.

Lo'lei high, Lo'lei low.
They got that Lo'lei by her toe.
Got home, can't get to bed.
Memories, dancing in her head.
Tie Lo'lei to that mast,
For all the purging of the past.
Momentum swings, left then right,
Don't let that noose get too tight.

The boys look up from peering into the camera.

"It's a work of art, dats what it is," Brooks bellows.

"TV weathergirl royalty," Myles sighs. "How does royalty come to stumble around in the mud with us and still walk with grace?" he adds.

"A grace dat defies," Brooks growls. "Burn bright, Lorelei. Never shy away from the light."

"Oh, shut up the pair of you and get a room," Lorelei interrupts. "Put this note in the envelope with the tape. Let's make the forecast happen."

====//====

Going as the Three Stooges was Brooks's idea. *Three lowbrow lunkheads........we'll fit in perfectly*, he said. It is also a two-fingered gesture to the church......*we'll show 'em who the stooges re-*

ally are! The "Hark Now Hear Momentum Sing" Christmas Fundraiser was a "Famous Face Ball" and the ticket promised, for a hundred dollar donation, an evening of spiritual and seraphic revelry. We arrive fashionably late (under the instruction of Myles) and the event is already in full flow. Ethan, or should I say Bing Crosby, peels off to talk to another Momentum crony who is sporting a Stevie Wonder mask, complete with dreadlocks.

The Christmas carol, I Saw Three Ships (Come Sailing In), is being harmonised by a choir in one corner of the large room.

"Three fuckin' ships! Fuckoutahea!" Brooks, through his Moe mask, mutters loudly. Ronald Reagan turns in disgust, but Moe continues regardless.

"Deys in the desert! Fuckin' ships?! I tell yous."

"Shhh, don't bring attention to us," Myles, aka Curly, beseeches. Lorelei, who is struggling to see through her Larry camouflage, chips in.

"It's camels, you dope. The ships are camels."

Brooks and Myles have goofball expressions on their masks, which makes any serious conversion piece look ludicrous. Lorelei scans the room. In fact, it is difficult to take anything seriously. Marilyn Monroe is chatting to Charlie Chaplin to our left, whilst Brad Pitt and someone who could only be Jesus Christ chew the fat to our right. JFK is remonstrating with Charles Manson, whilst Davy Crockett argues the toss in a 3-way face-off with Miss Piggy and the little bloke from the Love Boat.

"Eyes on da prize," is all that Brooks says, at once bringing our objective back into focus. This is going to be one bizarre evening. And I can only hope a fateful one, at that. My words reverberate inside Lorelei's skull.

I think it's time we got you home, don't you.

====//====

I am pretty normal. I have a job, a wife and two children. I live in comfort in a house just big enough to cope, but too small to fully satisfy. A comfortable life. Normal. Yeah, that's it, normal. But normal comes at a cost. Somebody once said that normal is for people without any courage. My brother's life is not normal. He is courageous enough to seize every damn opportunity that presents itself in his abnormal life. Changing jobs, sleeping with random women, spontaneous acts of generosity, unique holidays. And through this maelstrom, his beaming face persists. It's just not fair. I swear he could stop the sun rising if he never wanted the party to end.

The Three Stooges edge their way through the incongruous throng of famous faces towards the dais where the 'collection box' is housed. Brooks takes a huge wad of notes from his inside pocket and shares them with Myles and Lorelei, counting out five hundred dollars each. Myles then asks a man in a Zorro mask to take a photo of them on his smartphone "donating to the cause". We gather round the unremarkable steel box and pose in a proud-to-be-supporting-such-a-worthy-cause kind of way.

"Take 3 or 4, just in case I blink," Myles asks the black-masked legend.

"You guys look just great. I hope you Stooges are smilin' under there."

"Fuk-an-ay-rite, we're smiling, buddy," Brooks spits from behind his Moe façade.

Zorro hands back the phone and turns to engage with a female rocking a Kardashian mask, just don't ask me which one. Our bundles of cash are almost ceremonially tossed into the box and I can't help but notice an unmistakably Mel-shaped Barney Rubble staring at Lorelei intently. We Three Stooges, our fiscal responsibilities over for the moment, disperse back into the partying crowd and Mel's gaze is stymied by a new congregation of masks.

Shirley Temple offers to read Lorelei's palm. Myles exits the scene with a wink. It's time for him to start his work for the evening. Shirley is quite obviously an older woman, despite wearing the mask and curls of an eight-year old, and the voice really doesn't match the face. Lorelei accepts the invitation nonetheless. After all, she has some time to kill. Brooks watches on intently.

"Do you want to know your future?" Shirley asks.

I do.

"I do," repeats Lorelei quietly. Shirley takes both of Lorelei's hands into hers and begins.

"The church will tell you that the best way to create a future you're happy with is to take consistent, positive action every day. But I like a little dabble on the metaphysical side of life..........mmm, water hands." She holds Lorelei's hands, palms up, and continues.

"People with water hands are really emotional. Are you searching for peace, darling?" Shirley asks.

"I guess so."

"Thought as much. Short, oval palm. Flexible fingers, quite long. I'd wager that you are an artistic girl. Am I correct?"

"Maybe."

"But you get stressed out. You get too hooked up in those feelings of yours, eh?"

Lorelei shoots a nervous smile.

"Now let me see your left hand first. You see, this hand shows your potential. The other one tells me what you've done with that potential."

"I see."

"You see this line?" Shirley runs her finger across horizontally just below the fingers. "That's your heart line, right there. See where it starts?"

"Kind of between my index and middle finger. Does that mean something?"

"It sure does, honey. You fall in love a little too easily, I think."

I can feel Lorelei redden slightly.

"There's also a little circle or some kind of interruption. See there?" She points to a blemish near the middle of the palm. "Have you had it tough in love? That tells me some kind of emotional trauma, you know like sadness or depression."

Lorelei simply nods. Shirley goes on.

"The next line down. That, my dear, is your head line."

"She ain't fond of headlines, ma'am" I'd almost forgotten Brooks was standing behind us.

"Well, it's curvy. That means you're a creative girl. And spontaneous, probably. Maybe that's why you fall in love too easy," Shirley chuckles.

"And why I'm a mess," replies Lorelei matter of factly. Shirley continues regardless.

"Your life line. Here. Well, it's quite short and shallow."

"What does that mean?" asks Lorelei nervously.

"You are extremely easily manipulated by others."

"That's why I'm here." She looks back to her palm.

"See this line here," Shirley ploughs on. "This is your fate line. Read this and your life line together, well, that's your future right there, honey."

"I hope it's good news."

Shirley adjusts her golden locks and stares intently at Lorelei's lines.

"That fate line looks pretty deep to me."

"That's funny, because I'm sure it never used to be that pronounced," Lorelei admits.

"You're in the hands of destiny, my girl. And do you see those breaks in the line? External forces will change your life many times."

"Really?" Lorelei's eyes widen. Brooks gives her a gentle squeeze on her shoulder.

I am rather hoping that internal forces will change her life, and my death, just the once, thank you.

====//====

Myles eventually appears in the entrance to the church and gives us the thumbs-up sign.

"Fuckin' A," Brooks spits. Lorelei takes a deep breath.

"Yeah, fuckin' A-bout time."

Brooks leans in and whispers, "I love it when you talks doirty."

"Let's get this thing done, Mr Brooks."

Lorelei walks over to the entrance to where Myles is standing. He smiles nervously.

"Oh my. I have goosebumps on my goosebumps. I thought I would never find the same box. Nothing at Ace. Couldn't get a match at True Value. Then Logans came up trumps."

"Well done. You're a true hero," Lorelei reaches forward and kisses Myles on the cheek. I just hope that the sight of two of the three stooges kissing hasn't drawn attention to us.

"Thank you. You are a sweetheart. The box is just around the corner. I've put *the tape* in there too. Oh my, I haven't been this nervous since 9th Grade Prom night," Myles says breathlessly.

"Just create *the* best distraction ever and I'll love you forever."

"Oh well, here goes nothing," Myles turns and heads towards Brooks on the opposite side of the church hall, through the multitude of masks. Lorelei slips out of sight and breathes, barely audibly, "I think it's time I got me home."

====//====

Brooks is nursing a bruised eye but is still grinning from ear to ear.

"I still don't know why ya had to hit me that hard!"

Myles is in the back of the car organising passports and tickets, whilst also counting the money from the brimming box, replete with dollar bills.

"It was the only way, besides, I think I probably owed you one."

"For what?"

"Oh my. For plenty."

"Now, now, boys, let's make sure we get to the airport in one piece, please. It's much better to be a live anecdote than a dead statistic."

"Amen to dat, sweet-pea."

The church was in absolute chaos. Brooks shouted loudly at a wholly innocent Abraham Lincoln. Myles interjected with a swinging right hook, knocking his Stooge brother to the ground. Michael Jackson jumped on Myles's back, which Brooks, inexplicably to the shocked throng, took offence to. The ensuing altercation engaged approximately half the room but more importantly, occupied every masked eye there. Lorelei strolled up to the dais and within 20 seconds had completed the switch and was waiting in the car park for the disgraced Stooges to appear a minute or two later.

With Ethan's car keys in Lorelei's clutch bag, the getaway surely had to be smoother than any Keystone Cop episode. As none of the Stooges owned a car, this was where Ethan fitted in. They weren't exactly stealing his car, merely borrowing it for the evening. Besides, Ethan had volunteered his services hadn't he? The fact that he was under Lorelei's supremely acted spell is simply supposition, m'Lud.

As Brooks would have it, "Amen to dat, sweet-pea."

====//====

"Don't let anyone rent a space in your head unless they're a good tenant." – Anon

I didn't realise that Timbuktu was a real place until the fellow from Fiji told me about the man from Mali. It also hadn't really occurred to me that there might be 'others' in the same situation as me. I was lucky in finding a body on a cruise ship in the middle of the Atlantic. I guess that there will be Chinamen in South America and vice versa, struggling with language barriers until they 'touch off' into another like-speaking soul. Maybe I thought I *was* the only one. The fellow from Fiji put me right about that too.

Lorelei's connection at LAX from Washington was seamless, in spite of her obvious nervousness. She had around two hours to kill before our flight to Sydney. Once security and border control had been negotiated safely and without alarm, Lorelei, went 'underground' just like her weathergirl character, hiding in a toilet cubicle for over an hour.

Arriving at the gate late and when boarding the plane, Lorelei could not help the odd circumspect glance over her shoulder. Only when the plane was finally in the air, after taxiing for what seemed like hours, could she fully relax. She turned to her right and smiled at the man in seat 38B, a wiry African man in casual travelling clothes reading a Lonely Planet guide to "Australie". Elbows touch on the shared arm rest and I decide to swap seats, after all, it will be a long flight and

I will have plenty of time to exchange bodies back again before we land.

Whoooosh!!.

Straight away it felt a little different. Occupying a female host had the same vibe as being inside a male, so gender was not the issue. This was a question of space. Or, more specifically, the lack of it. It was then that the fellow from Fiji introduced himself. Well, it was not so much an introduction as an all-out assault.

"Taro-va! Biuti au tu madaga! Who the hell are you?"

"What the....?"

"Get out of here. This is my territory. Mine. Please leave. I don't want any trouble here, mister."

The soul sparring continued for a while until civility kicked in and we began to talk and ask questions of each other. Jeet was, once upon a living time, a gardener in Thurston Gardens in Suva when he was struck by lightning. One minute he was tending to some Tahitian Gardenias, the next he was stumbling through the desert, with not a plant or flower in sight. His Malian host was apparently fleeing the Ansar Dine, an Islamic fundamentalist group, who he had somehow pissed off, and ended up roaming the desert in Northern Mali living a nomadic lifestyle. He's been travelling ever since that day.

"So, you just died, mister?" Jeet asks.

"No, I've been dead for a little while now," I reply matter-of-factly.

"But you have only just arrived. Were you in, how do you say, purgatory?"

"You could say that but, no, I've had a number of hosts since my death."

"How can this be?"

"Look to your left. See her. That is my latest host."

"But........" Jeet sounds perplexed.

"I move from host to host."

"But how?"

"Through touch. She touched him. I became your new lodger."

"But......" Jeet splutters.

"Don't worry, I'll go back into her soon," I try and reassure Jeet. "I'll leave you in peace."

"Thank you. What is it they say in the films? This town ain't big enough for the both of us."

"For some reason, I thought I was the only one. Do you think he can hear us?" I ask.

"Maybe yes. But he can't understand us. He speaks French. *Very leetle England*! I haven't really spoken to anyone in years. Please excuse my rust, mister"

"Then how do you control him? Well, I assume you know that you can influence your host a little." Our voices echo dully in the now-crowded void, but there is an explicit clarity when he says simply.

"I hijack his dreams, silly."

====//====

I am at the lake when I tell Maddy that I'm leaving her. Except Maddy is not there. She is at home dealing with another pseudo crisis with the girls. I call in the middle of a Barbie-down-the-toilet episode and I can't suppress a giggle when she tells me what has happened. Bad move.

So, I am at the lake when I tell Maddy that I'm leaving her.

Except I don't actually tell Maddy that I'm leaving her because the words don't leave my mouth. The mute storm before the calm. Mother Nature then proceeds to heckle my non-declaration. Despite a vast sky to explore, a host of starlings begin their murmur, their mesmerizing dusk dance, in front of me. They wheel and pivot, soar and swoop. Like flames, they leap and dance, and for the length of their early evening acrobatics, I am in their thrall. More and more enter the shape-shifting ballet, huddling and hurtling together, safety in numbers to counter predatory raids. They survive by being together. My idea of survival is to be apart. I take in their veering choreography for a few seconds more and then head for the car, Maddy already having hung up on the voiceless me.

====//====

"Are you ready, mister?"

"Ready as I'll ever be."

"Let us go on a journey inside his dream. Keep up." Jeet has already disappeared, whirring to the front part of the man from Mali's mind.

"We wait until the eyes start to tremble," Jeet whispers. "That is when the dreaming starts. And that is when we make our move. What do you want him to do?"

"I have no idea," I say, scratching my virtual head. "I don't know what would work."

"OK, look at it like this. You can see all of his memories behind, right?"

"Yes."

"Dreams do not cause new memories. They draw on old memories. You can't dream something you don't know."

"I guess not."

"Dreams are the *experience* of new memories being created. Like east meeting west. Firing and wiring. New mental associations. That's it. You disrupt the dream with something new, like a new memory, and the memory bank goes crazy. Like I said, dreams don't normally cause new memories. When they do, the brain treats it like a portent of the future. He thinks it must have some sort of meaning and be acted on. Like creating a new shopping list."

"But how do you add something new into a dream?"

"Have you ever acted before?" Jeet responds with another question.

"Not really, just school plays and the like."

"Just be you. Come on, let's have some fun. His eyes are starting to move. Let's go mister."

We enter a desert scene with a difference. On the face of it, it seems fairly typical. Date palms stare silently at the sun. Overhead, buzzards survey the scene, looming dark shapes in the neon blue sky. There is colour in this dream. And sounds too, the bustle of the scene seeping through eventually, like someone slowly turning the volume button. Then there is the smell: a bubbling brew of burning sand; smoky wafts of grilled food; fetid body odour; and, pervading almost everything, death. There are men dressed head-to-toe in ominous black, inky shadows dotted around the dazzling arena. They stand and observe the white-robed men taking part in some form of triple jump competition. However, there is no runway for these desert athletes, merely more sand, making their run-ups almost impossible. There is a line, quite literally a line in the sand that they have to land in advance of. Failure means being chased by one of the men in black. Exit stage right to heaven knows what.

"Just act normal," Jeet murmers.

"What on earth.....?" Dreams are weird, everyone knows that, but until you are actually standing inside one, you will never get a sense of the true irrational absurdity of one.

We stand by one of the hawker stalls selling street food that line the event. Skewers of sheep eyes stare at us from the grill as a faceless man plucks more bounty from a bleating ewe behind the stall. Almost everybody in the scene is faceless. They are either blurred or so non-descript as to render them faceless to everyone anyway.

"What do we do now?" I ask.

"Whatever you want, my friend. It seems scary, but remember that you never die in your dreams. He'll be wakey-wakey before that happens. Try something," Jeet implores.

I pick the sheep eyes off the nearest skewer and throw them one by one in our host's direction. He turns and faces me, fear and loathing etched in his features. He begins to run away, in the direction of the line in the sand. His first attempt. He gains very little traction, the sand is so soft, inducing a series of stumbles. The first line draws closer and he has no momentum whatsoever.

"Come on, let's help him a little, eh?" Jeet remarks, pulling me to the side of the dream. I hear a loud whistle. It is Jeet, summoning the giant buzzards overhead. They approach noiselessly and hover above us. Jeet motions towards the struggling man from Mali and they ascend accordingly. They stall in the desert breeze, then plunge downwards rapidly at an angle to elevate Mali from one line to beyond the other. One hawker claps excitedly, the faceless black robes stare. Mali keeps running.

"Come on," Jeet beckons. We appear on the horizon, looking back at the scene.

"Can I do *anything*?"

"Give it a try, mister."

"Let's bring a piece of Sydney to the desert, then." I think about one of the greatest views in the world – Sydney harbour. Nothing happens.

"What's the problem?"

"I, err, don't know how to do it." I reply.

"What are you trying to do, mister?"

"See Sydney harbour. Over there." I point over at the horizon. Mali, meanwhile, is still toiling in the blistering heat to our left.

"Then you really have to feel it, not just see it. And I mean feeeeeel it."

I try again. I draw on my memories, my first visit to Sydney, seventeen years old, the hope invested in summer's infancy, Opera House sails like waratah petals pressed on a stirring sapphire sky, Harbour bridge leaching grey into everything around it..........I'm feeeeeeeeling it.

The whole aspect and panorama of the dream changes. We are no longer at ground level. We find ourselves standing on the uppermost section of the bridge's famous arch, overlooking a harbour of..........sand. Boats are replaced by a flotilla of camels. The man from Mali is with us, surveying the spectacle, breathing easier, a wondrous smile forming on his lips.

"There, I told you it was easy."

"Wow."

"You've created a new memory for him. I have a feeling that he'll head straight for Sydney harbour when we land. Climbing the Bridge will be too hard to resist," Jeet smiles.

It is time to say goodbye to Jeet, to vacate his space. I want to thank him for the experience, for exhibiting new clues, for being part of my journey, for being like me. But I'm already gone, the barest touch, propelling me back into a dozing Lorelei.

====//====

When I was a teenager, I used to lie with Michael under the covers. Sometimes it was my bed we would squeeze into – of course, Michael got first choice of bed, the biggest, usually. We would talk late into the night, the covers providing a sufficient screen to keep unwanted noise in. We would talk about anything and everything and I remember one night Michael talking about death. He said that he knew what happened to people when they died. After they are buried, they get to wait around in this big room, with tea and coffee and cake, which is all very nice for a while, but it soon gets a touch tedious.

You see, Michael explained to my willing ears, you only get to leave the room, die fully to be exact, when your name is mentioned for the very last time. I remember asking where they went after this, but Michael said that nobody knew exactly where, whether it was a better place or worse. I said I wanted to be remembered by lots of people because tea and cake for ages and ages sounded OK to me, but Michael said it sounded like purgatory. I didn't know what that meant, although I'm beginning to feel I understand that word a little better now.

====//====

"Are the dead as lonesome as the living?" – Truman Capote

"Plane food doesn't have to be plain food."

He writes in a spiral reporter pad and sits back, saying aloud, "yeah, that should do it." He then opens the top drawer of his desk to reveal an oval mirror on which sit six perfectly straight parallel lines of white powder. There is a rolled up note residing next to the small, hand-sized mirror, which is soon re-rolled and inserted up his right nostril. The left-hand line disappears and I'm marooned in a whiteout for a few seconds. When the blizzard abates, all I hear is, "Good gear, good gear." The drawer snaps shut and he starts to write again.

"Tell me, dear readers, the two attributes that sweet and sour pork should attain to. Enough time? Well, it was neither. And I sincerely hope it was pork. And while we're at it. Don't ever wrestle with a pig. You'll both get filthy, but only the pig will be happy about it. Which is more than can be said for eating in Airports......."

"And I sincerely hope it *was* pork," he repeats a sentence from his recent scrawl. And again, but this time with a different emphasis, "And I sincerely *hope* it was pork." He throws his pencil down on the desk and leans back in his battered director's chair. He lets out a snort.

"Like it matters. Like it really matters, JJ. No fucker is reading me nowadays anyway." And with that, he opens the drawer again and demolishes another poodle's leg. He begins to scribble some more, faster and faster, barely legible by the end.

"It was Frederick Mercury that penned, "Don't stop me now. I'm having such a good time, I'm having a ball." Well, I've just had a thai fish ball and I'm certainly not having a good time. I digress. Serving myself, yes, that's right readers, they don't serve you, I bumped into a lady and spilled her soup over her. I can hear you Mr. Mercury. "Two hundred degrees – that's why they call me Mr Fahrenheit." Maybe it should be Mr Centigrade, because the dish was so luke-warm, she didn't even yell out in pain. Which got me thinking. I understand that the word 'luke' comes from the Middle English 'leuk' which, in turn, was borrowed from the Dutch 'leuk' meaning 'tepid'. Since tepid means 'barely warm' there was no reason to add 'warm' to 'luke' in 'lukewarm'! Warm is redundant. A bit like this excuse of an airport restaurant."

The room is small, the floor strewn with newspaper cuttings, the bookcase against one wall overfed with cookbooks and magazines, with only the desk manifestly tidy. On the wall opposite the bookcase is a letterbox-shaped painting of Da Vinci's The Last Supper, adjacent to a plaque stating, "J.J. Lowe – Legend In His Own Lunchtime." There is also a heady smell in the air, a cocktail of cheap after-shave and marijuana. This is where I have ended up. Geographically, I am closer to home, but somehow I still feel a million miles away. We stare at The Last Supper. I'm not sure even Jesus can help me here.

====//====

I may have said that love and, what I really mean is in particular, sex at the beginning of a relationship is much like chemistry. Two separate and distinct concoctions being mixed together to create a unique, exciting, heady brew.

I've changed my mind. It's much more akin to art. Head-spinning beauty, mind-blowing creativity, the uniqueness and newness of it all. Just like a challenging piece of art, you cannot even describe it, never mind try to understand it.

So, what begins as art turns, over time, to a wholly different beast – the discipline of science. When you do X and I do Y, Z happens. Press whatever button needs pressing and bingo, stuff happens. It's about as creative as cooking with a microwave. It's not just the sex, it's our relationship too. Same rules apply.

Maybe the masterpiece of Maddy and me is now finished, the paint well and truly dried, worn and old, observed by a thousand eyes, nothing more to be read into it.

====//====

The switch took me by surprise. Lorelei refrained from eating on the flight (anxiety? plane food? sleep?), so as soon as immigration was surmounted and the green, nothing-to-declare aisle traversed, she scurried into a no-frills Asian eatery in the Arrivals hall. She chose the tom yam soup and was returning to her seat when a gentleman leaving the restaurant barged into her causing half the contents of her soup (I'm not sure if it was tom or yam) to capsize over her. The expected profusion of apologies was forthcoming and in the middle of one "I'm so sorry, let me help you with that", I was gone. The gentleman continued to apologise but the touching had ended. I was housed in another host, watching my previous host diminish in size as we walk further and further away.

====//====

Sunday 15th May

Michael came round today. I think Maddy likes him more than me. I caught them whispering in the kitchen over something or other. Thing is, I wouldn't put it past him. I thought siblings were supposed to stick together in adversity. Jeez, I'm getting paranoid. It was probably nothing. At least the Demons got home in the final quarter today.

====//====

"How dare he write such a good review."

"Is the food that bad there?"

"No, not at all. No, it's his writing which is so damned good. In fact, his words are always more palatable than the food he's writing about. I hate him. Look."

"If being nerdy is just being extremely passionate, obsessed even, about something, then call me a food nerd. There I've said it, readers. I am a nerd."

"I called him a nerd once, because of that stupid fucking sweater he wore at that photo shoot. And he gets to write that in response. Shitbag."

"Look, JJ, you only got this gig because we go back. I still think you're the best food critic, period."

"I am not a food critic, Arlo. I love food, it's the restaurants that fuck it up I mainly have issues with," JJ cuts in. The Editor holds his hands up in mock surrender.

"OK, I stand corrected. You're the best restaurant critic around. But,......" he pauses.

There's always a but, isn't there?

"......circulation figures haven't improved since you've been on board and you're hardly pulling up trees at the focus groups we've conducted."

"Is that why you called me in here? Am I jumping or being pushed?"

The Editor is taken aback a little.

"No, I've got a 5-day assignment for you. Take a friend. Enjoy the food, enjoy the company. You're looking a little strung out, JJ." He hands over an envelope.

There is a long pause before JJ responds.

"Can you handle a bit of controversy?"

"I don't like the sound of this."

"Let's put it this way, a bit of beef with the only other food critic in town might see the temperature in the kitchen rising a little."

"And this quarter's readership figures rising like a soufflé too, I hope."

JJ chuckles. "Leave it to me. This is going to get tasty." JJ turns to leave.

"Hey, don't cross the line. Just remember where the lines are, my friend."

"I never forget where the lines are," JJ winks and exits the Editor's office, unopened envelope in hand.

====//====

I go foraging for images or recollections inside JJ's recesses. I push and probe. Smells rise above the surface, wafting down neural corridors. It's a mess in here, memories scattered every-where, mostly masked by clouds of white. I get an urge to tidy up. Well, I have got to live in here too. I start sorting through the debris. Snorting through the debris would be more appro-priate, mind you. I separate the smells from their associated memories, pushing the former down an ingress near the frontal lobe and leaving the latter stockpiled in the corner. Well, it's a start anyway. I will continue the spring clean later.

It is not long before JJ smells a rat. Or doesn't, as the case may be. He prepares a salad of Serrano ham, smoked mozzarella and balsamic figs – a true lunch with a punch. Instead of a barrage on the buds, he gets nothing. He starts muttering to himself.

"Not much smokiness in this cheese...............mmm, these figs........i shouldn't need more balsamic dressing to balance the sweetness...............actually, what sweetness?..........these figs are bland.............shit............what the fuck..........."

Dinner is no better. A bland bouillabaisse does not serve up groans of delight, merely groans.

"What is going on in my mouth?" is all JJ can muster. He calls his doctor and arranges an appointment for the morning. I pilfer and plunder his head some more as he sleeps, remem-bering to tidy up as I go. I may even try and tinker with his dreams, unless they are shrouded in white as well.

====//====

Monday 16th May

My birthday! Turns out the cloak-and-dagger whispering was Maddy and Michael finalising plans for my birthday. I feel bad now. I am officially an idiot. I LOVE LOVE LOVE my present. I LOVE LOVE LOVE my wife. I must stop fearing the worst in everything.

====//====

JJ knocks on the door loudly four times and then enters the room without waiting for a response.

"Oh, just come in anyway. Lucky I wasn't testing my doctor-patient relationship credentials. You really wouldn't want to see my real bedside manner now, would you?" the grey-bearded man jokes.

JJ takes one of the two chairs on the opposite side of the doctor's desk. The room is full of the usual doctor's surgery paraphernalia – an examination table, extra chairs, some random toys, eye charts and how to quit smoking posters.

"Sit down, why don't you?"

"Just tell me the bad news, Phil."

"It's hardly life-threatening. You appear to have lost your sense of taste."

"Hardly life-threatening?!? It's an un-fucking-mitigated disaster, that's what it is," JJ rails. "I'm a fucking food critic. With no sense of taste. Yeah, that's going to work." He stands up and starts to pace around the room.

"Can you not write about something else?"

"What?!?"

"You can still write, can't you? Maybe try a motoring column or travel. You like travelling, don't you?"

JJ ignores him and goes on regardless. "Is this a permanent thing? I mean, if it's just come on suddenly, it can disappear quickly too, right?"

"Look, JJ, it's not as simple as yes or no."

"We go back a long way, Phil. I'm in a bit of a pickle here."

"Go on."

"I've got an assignment for the paper. Five restaurants in five days, all around the country. If I can't taste anything, then I'm fucked, pardon my French."

"Calm down. The way I see it, you've got three choices. Number one, you cancel. I'll write you some sort of doctor's note saying you're too unwell to travel. Don't worry, you're tasteless secret will be safe with me."

"Ha fuckin' ha."

"Number two, you go on the trip regardless and, how can I put it.......wing it. Make something up. You *can* still write after all."

"Or, last but by no means least, you get someone else to taste the food for you and you write about that. After all, who's to say that their opinion of the fare is no less worthy than yours?" Doctor Phil says unconvincingly and adds, "Except you, maybe."

"Hardly a bottomless pit of options I've got, is it?" JJ looks doleful, gloom replacing lids being flipped, before asking, like an afterthought.

"I suppose you're not free next week are you, Phil?"

I suspect JJ is not even expecting an answer, never mind the one that Phil gives.

"As a matter of fact, I had planned to take a couple of days off before Christmas. Myself and a colleague were tossing up how to divide the holiday period up. The practice gets so very quiet at this time of the year and we can legitimately have a skeleton staff on."

JJ is still processing the information. Phil continues regardless.

"I'd love to. Thank you for inviting me. I won't let you down. I've always fancied getting paid for eating."

"Who said anything about getting paid! Look, I could possibly stretch to expenses," JJ says unconvincingly.

"Count me in." And with that, Doctor Phil gets to his feet, shakes JJ's hand and escorts us to the door.

"Let me know the details, as soon as," Phil says, shutting the door behind him, leaving JJ looking rather bewildered in the empty waiting room.

In the descending lift, JJ finally opens the envelope, unfolds the paper and reads.

To : J J Lowe
From : Messenger Editorial
Re : Themed Restaurant Trip
Date : 15th December

For our New Year special, we thought it a good idea to look at Australia's most quirky restaurants. The term "Modern Australian" has variously been known as international, mod-oz, fusion or contemporary, and denotes a culinary culture that is the result of a collision of cuisines from around the world. But, how can we be even more modern? Is the experience of eating equally as important? Or is it just about the food? We are sure that you will let us know, JJ.

So, we've made reservations for you (plus one guest) at some of the best experiential restaurants in Australia. [See itinerary below].

Enjoy the food, enjoy the experience more. And write well. Better than that bastard Starczewski, anyway.

Monday – Nova – Lime Street, Sydney

[Outer Space themed restaurant, where fine dining provides as immersive a space experience as any thrill-park ride]

Tuesday – Nubilous – Banks Street, Brisbane

[Dining in the dark takes you on a journey of taste that will enhance your world of senses]

Wednesday – Food for Thought – Carnegie Walk, Melbourne

[An immersive interactive dinner performance where your meal is the ultimate three-act drama and where true gastronomy resembles a vibrant symphony for the senses]

Thursday – Rock Paper Scissors – Adams Street, Adelaide

[You know the game, right? You win - You choose - You pay. We win - We choose - We pay. Simple.]

Friday – Tale Knows – Forster Parade, Perth

[Celebrating the age old tradition of using every part of the animal, serving up the inner organs of beasts in mind-blowing dishes that combine high sophistication with peasant simplicity.]

We look forward to seeing your drafts – no later than the 28th please.

Regards,
 Editorial

====//====

My focus fixes on Wednesday and my virtual heart leaps. I even do one of those comedic double-takes you see in the cartoons. I read the spiel again in case I have made a mistake. Food for Thought. Maddy's sister works in Food for Thought! I remember her telling me about the concept of food theatre. To be honest, I barely listened, preferring instead to replay strained conversations with Maddy over and over in my head. But I remember the name clearly. Food for Thought. There can only be one, surely. What are the odds?!? If I can somehow get JJ to touch Ella, I could be home for Christmas. Ella always visits on Christmas Day and I'm sure that this year will be no different. I'm doing cartwheels inside JJ's head.

I'm going home!
I'm going home!
I'm going home!

"Fuck me, this stuff is strong," is JJ's response, as the lift doors open on the ground floor.

====//====

The main thing that can turn a relationship rancid, just like any festering wound, is time. They say that time is a great healer, that time cures everything. But for every action there is an equal and opposite reaction, right? Think about it. So, if time cures, it can also destroy. Old Father Time may have been wise, but Young Married Couple Time were at the back of the queue when wisdom was handed out. They find each other. In that moment, at the start of time itself, there is no more loneliness, no doubts or confusion. You complete each other. You become whole. And that magical feeling is called falling in love. And then the arc of time kicks in. The way you feel at the start of time itself, because you cannot remember a time before her, is unsustainable. Falling in love becomes just love, and all love ultimately affords us is a front-row seat on somebody else's flaws. And believe me, both Maddy and I had deep flaws.

====//====

JJ arranges to meet Doctor Phil at a wine bar two blocks away from the outer-space-themed restaurant. Considering it's a

Monday, the wine bar is relatively full, mainly with the suited and booted post-work crowd.

"Can I just say how excited I am for this week. Finally, I get to see how you work. Thank you for the invite, JJ."

"I think you'll find that you invited yourself."

Phil ignores this and continues. "How are those taste buds doing since I saw you last?"

"Still fucked," JJ is all dejection, sipping on his vodka and tonic. "Even this is like drinking tap water."

"Looks like I'll have to do a bit of work on this trip, then," Phil says unsympathetically.

"Just tell me if anything tastes shit and I'll handle the rest," JJ explains, rifling in his wallet. He pulls a credit card out and stands up.

"We off already?" Phil asks, starting to get up.

"No, I'm off to the toilet. Hold the fort."

Two minutes and one hastily devoured line later, we return. JJ rubs his nose and takes his seat again.

"You know doing *that* won't help you taste much, don't you?" Phil has his doctor hat on now.

"Can you keep your professional opinion to yourself for the next 5 days, please."

"Just saying."

"Well, don't."

"It's funny though, medically speaking, it all starts to go downhill around forty. That's when our taste buds begin to stop growing back, which means food starts to taste blander. My mother needs so much salt on her food...." JJ stops Phil in his tracks, holding his hand up.

"Enough already. I'm not dead yet. Besides, you apparently can't write properly until you're forty. Science the shit out of that, Doc."

"If we're spending the next five days together, maybe you can start being a little more civil. Critique the shit out of that, JJ."

JJ's smile turns into a full-bloodied laugh.

"OK, how is the lovely Judy? Still wearing the trousers in the household?"

"She's fine and, by the way," Phil strokes his grey beard, "we have a free and equal relationship. No upper hands or lower opinions. We are very happy. Even after nearly 30 years."

"Is it really that long? And you're still playing the field and getting away with it. You're a lucky man, Phil."

"Free and equal. Free and equal. Never forget that she is my harbour, JJ, the safe haven I always come back to. All the other dalliances are mere ports of call in a storm, transient places where I have no real affinity. I've told you before, sex and love are two different entities."

"You're a hell of a lucky man." JJ repeats, shaking his head. He goes on.

"And what I love most about you two is that you are a doctor and she is a judge. Doctor Phil and Judge Judy. You couldn't fucking make it up!" JJ splurts.

"Like a restaurant critic with no sense of taste. You just couldn't make it up, eh, JJ?" They both give way to laughter.

The wine bar is all industrial chic. Light bulbs encased in metal cages dangle from the ceiling while the stools, bar counter and bench in the middle of the room are all made from galvanised steel. Despite the décor, it somehow feels more like a 1970s wine and cocktail haunt than an industrial inner city bar.

"It makes a change, me not asking for a table for one."

"Yes, I hadn't really realised that you're the king of dining alone."

"It normally plays out like this. 'Table for one, please.' 'At one, for how many people?' 'No, a table for one person.' 'One?' 'Yes, one.' 'Ahh, OK. Mmmm, yes, we can squeeze you in.'" JJ shakes his head and repeats, "squeeze you in," with a sound of incredulity.

"Then they shoehorn you in a corner somewhere, well out of the way, I mean the sad bastard obviously doesn't want to be seen dining alone, does he?" JJ is on a roll. "And when the Maitre D or Chef spots who the sad bastard actually is, a table large enough for four miraculously appears in a prime spot near the window overlooking the beautifully-lit gothic cathedral or a pristine fucking lake. So, yes, I guess I am the king of dining alone."

"It obviously takes a special type of person," Phil offers.

"I am an only child, remember."

"Spoilt rotten, no doubt."

"Not at all. Never had anything, never wanted for anything."

"Ah, the usual sob story."

"You know it's a load of old bull what they say about only children."

"Like what?"

"That they have problems sharing things."

"Well it makes sense."

"You know that Jesus was an only child?"

"Oh God, where is this one going?"

"And you could never say he had a problem sharing, could you?"

"What about you? You always eat alone. Have you got problems sharing? I think I should be told."

JJ stands up and grabs his coat from the back of his chair.

"That's for me to know and you to find out these next few days."

====//====

We used to belong to a book club. We would meet once a month to discuss a book that had been chosen at the finale of the previous get-together. By the time our local bookshop had ordered in the 12 or so copies the group required, there left only 3 weeks to devour, ruminate and cogitate before our next book club evening.

Reading between the Wines (oh, how we laughed when Richard came up with that one) was the name we gave our little first-world monthly gathering. Some of the group (mainly Richard and Emma) only really turned up for the drinking. They felt the Book Club was a legitimate excuse to get hammered on a school night. Binge drinking, rather than cringe thinking. Which is what people like Pablo, Hannah and, to a certain extent, Maddy did, taking themselves a little too seriously and practically producing a whole thesis on that month's potboiler. I lay somewhere in between, absorbing a couple of glasses of the Barossa Valley's finest whilst giving (always salient) opinions and thoughts on theme, plot and characters. So, I enjoyed reading, but as Frank Zappa said, " So many books, so little time."

====//====

"An unexamined life is not worth living." – Socrates

I expected something very different from Nova. As JJ and Phil are shown to their table, there are no dancing Martians or waiters dressed as aliens. It looks like a run-of-the mill fine dining restaurant. JJ and Phil seem impressed.

"Thank fuck it's not gimmicky," JJ grunts, arranging the napkin on his lap.

"Yes, I was a little worried it would be Saturn sangas washed down with a Cosmos-politan," Phil giggles.

"Or a Mars-tini."

"We might still be in for a stellar evening, then!"

The waiter returns with a menu which includes a description of the restaurant and what diners can expect from their evening experience.

"A molecular fusion of astronomy and gastronomy, no less," Phil says, pointing to the line on the menu.

"There's real meteorite on the menu! Thank Christ my taste buds have packed up," JJ retorts.

"What?"

"They use real meteorite dust. Christ on a bike."

"Sounds interesting. Would you write that up as a good thing or bad thing?"

"It all depends how the evening plays out. It's all about building blocks, my friend."

"Now you've lost me. I'm sure you'll correct that, though."

"Welcome. Ambience. Menu. Service. Food. Experience. Like a pyramid. You have to start with a flat surface, though. No pre-conceptions. Or else the pyramid will be on shaky ground before we even start. I tend not to read other reviews about the place either. A clear mind leads to clear truths." JJ remarks smugly.

"Shall we go for the tasting menu? Full 5-courser?" Phil asks.

"Of course, when one is not picking up the bill, that is exactly what one does. Aperitif?" JJ is already thumbing through the drinks menu.

The waiter returns and JJ requests a Vernal Equinox, whilst Phil chooses a Gibbous Moon. Five-course tasting menu ordered, the waiter is dispatched and JJ pulls out a newspaper cutting from the previous day.

"Look at this, Phil. This is what I'm up against. The piece of Polish shit can write. Reckon I need to up my game."

Restaurant of the Week – Gilt - Roly Starczewski
"You don't need solid gold cutlery to eat 24-carat food. Yesterday,
I ate at Gilt and the only thing to feel guilty about was the price
at the end of the evening. It is said that perfection is achieved, not
when there is nothing more to add, but when there is nothing left
to take away. Like, let's say, on my empty plate."

"I've got my notebook ready whenever you want to start writing," Phil places a reporter's pad and pen next to his bread plate.

"Promise me one thing."

"What's that?"

"There's one word that you'll never write down. One word which I'm not allowed to use.......in any context. It will finish me off. For good."

"OK, what is it?"

"Promise?"

"Promise."

"Uranus."

They cackle at the naughtiness.

I dive to explore JJ's dark matter. There are arguments and tantrums, door-slammings galore. I enter one particularly dusty memory. There is a woman poking her head around a door, berating JJ. The words are not clear, but the sentiment behind them is written in bold.

"But Delia....," JJ repeats over and over.

The woman disappears leaving the door ajar. No door slam this time as JJ approaches and gently closes it. The memory lingers at funeral pace, just JJ standing on his own in a room.

I withdraw. JJ's eyes are firmly fixed on the menu he and Phil are now studying.

=-=-=-=-=-=-=

The Big Bang
maitake chawanmushi, toasted nori ficelles, ponzu lava

Atmosphe-re Entrée

xo-laminated bream, red claw yabbies, pomelo caviar stars

Total Eclipse
gnudi planets, kohlrabi, truffled chou-fleur, fermented garlic foam

Meteor Shower
robata lamb, fingerling potatoes, caramalised onion custard, meteorite dust*

Deep Space Dessert
saturn sapodilla, rose hip rings, long pepper ice cream, pomegranate asteroids

* Every particle is more than 4.5 billion years old and rich in minerals unknown on our planet. Along with otherworldly minerals, meteorite dust is also said to be packed with calcium, iron and magnesium.

=-=-=-=-=-=-=

Drinks arrive and they start to discuss the tasting menu. First up is the "Big Bang" course.

"Very clever," Phil admits.

"Let's hope it really is the start of something beautiful. Although I doubt it."

"You really are a glass-half-empty bloke, aren't you."

"Human nature. And personal experience."

"Ponzu lava."

"And the same to you."

"Thoughts, maestro?"

"Well, you know what they say, the proof of the pudding and all that."

"Well, it all looks very intriguing and eminently more impressive than I had feared. There's not a black hole burger in sight."

"Get your pen. Quick, I've got something for you."

"OK, fire away."

"Foam, go home."

"Nice."

"That's my opening gambit."

"But you haven't tasted anything yet."

"To be fair, I won't actually be tasting anything all evening, Phil."

"Good point, well argued."

"Just tell me whether anything is particularly amazing or gross and I'll conjure up some devastating wordplay to emphasise the point."

"I think I'm going to enjoy this evening. I actually feel like I'm eating in the future."

JJ rearranges the condiments for the third time and says.

"Phil. It's now, not new. Nothing is new. Everything has been done before, remember. It's deja-moo, that feeling you get when you've seen all the same bullshit before." A light bulb goes off in JJ's head. "Except for writing 'Lava palaver'. Jot that down while you're at it."

====//====

Friday 27ʰ June

We are now resorting to shadow boxing. Pretending to fight but not connecting with any punches. Also known as going through the motions. Surely the gloves are going to come off soon and Maddy is bound to win with a unanimous decision. Maybe that is what is needed to move things along here. Must remember to take my shirts to the dry cleaners.

====//====

The waiter brings dessert to the table. Phil gasps at its beauty and even JJ smirks at the representation of Saturn and its rings seemingly battered by asteroids on a large oval plate.

"Sir and sir, please. Here we have poached sapodilla, with rose hip, long pepper ice cream and pomegranate seeds," the waiter explains.

"Quite a sight," Phil adds.

JJ just continues to smirk.

"Please enjoy. And please, when you are finished, you are welcome to join us on the mezzanine to maybe look at the stars, a planet or two or even a distant galaxy. We have a forty-inch Monster Dobsonian telescope set up for your viewing experience. The clouds have officially parted and our resident astronomer is in the house," the waiter says with a flourish.

"Outstanding," Phil gasps, mouth wide open.

JJ utters a straightforward, "Thank you."

The waiter departs and Phil leans forward.

"What a place. You have to give this an amazing review."

"We'll see."

"It's been......it's been.....I've got it.......celestial," Phil leans back in his chair, pleased with himself.

"And you're talking out of........talking out of.......I've got it.......uranus."

"Objection, your Honour!"

"Overruled. OK, make a note of this instead," JJ snaps. He composes himself for a second, then starts. "Every meal should end with something sweet. It's like a post-mortem, it brings closure. The event horizon placed in front of us is of such visual magnitude, it's as if we are both blinded and warmed by the sun simultaneously."

"I like. I like."

"Even Roly Starczewski can't compete with that."

"You're an only child, remember, you're not supposed to be competitive. Play by the only child rules, JJ."

"Bullshit. I try to beat myself regularly. Therein lies the rub." JJ pauses, "Oh God, I *am* good at this wordplay lark."

Phil and JJ zestfully attack the dessert. Their eyes meet and Phil proffers a nod of gratification.

"Goooood," is all Phil can muster.

"If we were in space, you could murder me and nobody would know."

"How so?"

"In space no-one can hear ice cream."

"Groan."

"Keep eating, I'll check out the restrooms. It's important to tick the overall experience box. Got to complete the pyramid." Then almost imperceptibly, "A thick line should help hold it upright."

====//====

Maddy is a rug addict. Yes, you heard me correctly. It was game, set and match when she uttered the words, "Rugs connect us to our space. They complete not only the room, but the way you feel in it." It wasn't always like this. Like any addiction, she diligently went through all the phases. Experimentation first. Wool, natural fibre, cotton, synthetic, even hair-on-hide rugs came and went. Then came the regular use of rugs, every room had to house one and shopping trips became almost a weekly 'treat'. Problem or risky use of rugs is the next phase. When Maddy bought a huge shagpile Persian rug with gaudy gold and brown scrolls, I was suspicious. When she placed it in what was essentially a functional room (our study, for heaven's sake), then the alarm bells were ringing louder than the bang of the auctioneer's gavel that ushered in the sale in the first place. I feel we are now at the pure dependency or addiction phase. Rugs have taken hold and are the cause of changes in her mind and behaviour.

"Shut your eyes," she'd say if I ever commented.

If I did ever pluck up the courage to leave, maybe I would be replaced by a rug.

====//====

At the end of the evening, JJ goes into his study and rolls a joint. It is not long before he is talking to himself.

"Need to get some big zeds tonight. Busy day tomorrow. Better stack this," as he crumbles more of the brown block into the line of tobacco. I have two sleeps before Melbourne and a potential homecoming. I need to make sure it happens. I need to go dreamjacking.

JJ takes two pulls on the spliff, the first drawing air in, the second sending the heady mix deep into his lungs. A warm glow radiates as air passes through the fire, the effects eddying around his passageways. He transfers the cone to his left hand and picks up a pen with his right. He coughs.

"Whether you are on a two-man mission or dining Han Solo........."

"Fill up your inner space."

"One small step for man, one giant leap for restaurant kind."

Another big draw and JJ leans back in his director's chair. He sighs, smoke gushing from his mouth. A beam turns into a giggle.

"A space restaurant. And no fuckin' rocket in sight."

====//====

I infiltrate the dream. It has taken JJ a couple of hours to first drift off and, finally, to reach eye-darting REM dreamstate. I slip in unnoticed. If dreams are mostly about either wish-fulfillment or our greatest fears, I've entered one representing the former. JJ is flying, really flying. He's swooping and soaring over a town like an avian ballet dancer, moves administered with ease and flair. But this is no pas de deux. He dances alone, only the wispy clouds keep him company. There are no people on the ground either, no sign of life anywhere. I can see he is agitated, disturbed that he has no discernable audience to marvel at his balletic prowess. Stones appear in his hands and he flings them down at the houses, but there is still no response from the houses. More furious now, stones turn into larger rocks. Still no acknowledgement from ground level.

It is time to introduce Ella to his dream. This is where I have to concentrate, to really feel, according to Jeet. I try to conjure up her image but I struggle to remember what she looks like. I intensify my thoughts. Last Christmas, the lake, at Marco's party, up at the snow, when she used to babysit, that time I made her laugh. Yes, that's it. That time I made her laugh. Her face appears clear, defined, beautiful even. She ascends adroitly, willowy, a snapshot of elegance, until she reaches JJ. He looks surprised, but pleased. She hands him marshmallows to throw instead of the stones. They plunge together hand-in-hand. All fishdives and entrechats, they breathe their heady dance. The marshmallows fall into chimneys and land on doorsteps. People emerge in wonder. JJ looks at Ella and kisses the back of her hand in that old-fashioned way. They continue their descending dance, falling to earth, faster and faster. Ella suddenly mouths the word *goodbye* and is gone, leaving JJ alone, spiraling out of control towards the assembled crowds below. Closer, closer, closer........JJ flinches and sits bolt upright in bed, breathing heavily.

"That's some fucking gear," he gasps. JJ laboriously lies back, rolls over and awaits a potential second act with his heroine in the sky.

====//====

"How are the kids?"

We are in Brisbane. Heavy rain pummels the scene. The weather is not helping JJ's mood, which has been forbidding most of the day. He doesn't even look up as he answers Phil's question.

"Still sucking me dry."

JJ is holding the umbrella, one of those large corporate-logo golf types. Phil is getting drenched due to JJ's home-team favouritism, the umbrella positioned mostly above him. They scuttle into the canopied doorway of tonight's restaurant and JJ soaks Phil even more in the act of collapsing the umbrella.

"Let's get inside."

We flounder through the entrance and JJ is already extending his arm ready for someone to take the dripping umbrella. Thick black velvet curtains surround the passageway. A voice intonates from the semi-gloom.

"Good evening. Welcome to Nubilous. You must be the Lowe booking. Cassandra and Simone will guide you to your table. I hope you enjoy your evening."

"Guide?"

"Yes, let's say finding your table would be a little difficult on your own. It is dining in the dark, after all."

"Ok, guide away," Phil says as the two waitresses emerge into view. They are sporting pairs of what can only be infra-red goggles. Frankly, they look ridiculous.

"May I say that you look ridiculous," JJ bluntly concurs.

"Thank you," one of the girls says unconvincingly.

We are led behind the curtains into a place of sheer tenebrosity. No outlines, no gloom to peer through, just blackness. Low voices can be heard, whispering diners, everybody acutely aware that sound travels further in this atramentous terrain.

The girls locate our table and shepherd JJ and Phil into their seats. The clicking of heels indicates the waitresses have departed the scene.

"This is crazy," JJ breaks the silence, "I can't see my own nose."

"This could be fun," Phil giggles.

"God knows how you're going to write anything down for me, Phil."

"I thought of that."

"You would. Always the boy scout."

"I brought my Dictaphone."

"I hope you've brought your taste buds too. I'm in more trouble than the early settlers. No smell, no taste, no vision, no fucking hope. Great."

"How do we choose from the menu if we can't see it?"

"I hope that you don't mind, but I've sorted that out already. They are bringing us a selection. Chef's choice. Oh, and matching wines chosen by the sommelier. I don't normally do that as a critic. Not quite a level playing field, you see. But essentially it's the same as any other tasting menu, so I'll let it pass."

More clinking of heels as somebody approaches.

"Hello, it's Cassandra again. Please accept this little amuse bouche. Compliments of the chef."

"We'd love to," JJ answers. "What is it and, more importantly, where is it?"

"I'm going to turn our special lo-glo light on. You'll be able to see the outline of the food, but not the detail." A muted glow hovers over the table. Cassandra continues.

"Please enjoy chef's blue swimmer bonbons." With that, Cassandra's shadowy outline retreats.

"Bon appetite, mon brave," Phil offers.

"Et tu, brute," JJ replies.

Phil fumbles for cutlery, whilst JJ lunges in with his fingers.

"Wow, beautiful," Phil remarks, with his mouth still half full.

"Can't taste a thing. It may as well be confit de giraffe," sighs JJ.

I go for a meander. I am wondering whether Jeet was correct in saying that a new memory can be created by influencing a dream. I sift through JJ's catalogue. It doesn't take long for me to come across the flying Ella and I am comforted to see the resemblance straight away. He shouldn't have too much trouble recognizing her as the woman of his dreams when he claps eyes on her tomorrow. I hope. After all, she is now the absolute key to me returning home.

====//====

Sunday 6th August

If I were to be an actual part of Maddy, I would be her ribs. Close to her heart, but not quite close enough. Protecting her from outside forces, yet when that bond breaks, the pain is agony. It is hard to function with a broken rib. Even breathing is a chore. Time is the only healer, but does out of breath mean out of time?

====//====

JJ and Phil are having a hushed exchange in between courses.

"Did you see Roly's article about indigenous food today in the Sentinal?" Phil asks.

"See it? I've only had it rammed down my throat by him and his followers. Look at these." JJ extracates his mobile phone from his pocket. Turning it on bathes the whole table in a dull radiance. There are a stream of tweets, back and forth, between JJ and this Roly guy.

+++++++

JJLowe

Haven't we come further in the last 50,000 years than boiling up some leaves and calling it haute cuisine?

12 replies
357 retweets
55 likes

+++++++

+++++++

RolyPole

7hrsMore

@JJLowe How low can you go, Lowe? Best stick to your lambs fry and lamingtons.

38 replies
383 retweets
479 likes

+++++++

+++++++

JJLowe

6 hrs

@rolypole Ever thought why emu, dhufish and Geraldton wax haven't ever caught on?

18 replies
177 retweets
6 likes

+++++++

+++++++

RolyPole

6hrsMore

@JJLowe Embracing our culture and heritage should be higher on our culinary agenda. Not that you'd know much about culture.

75 replies
563 retweets
849 likes

+++++++

+++++++

JJLowe

5 hrs

@rolypole not that you'd know much about anything culinary, agendas or otherwise.....

31 replies
132 retweets
2 likes

+++++++

+++++++

RolyPole

5hrsMore

@JJLowe Wallaby critic or wannabe critic? You decide.

465 replies
968 retweets
1530 likes

+++++++

+++++++

JJLowe

4 hrs

@rolypole if you can't stand the heat get out of the bush kitchen……..

35 replies
92 retweets
3 likes

+++++++

+++++++

RolyPole
3hrsMore
@JJLowe Are you going to say sorry like Rudd? #loweblow
599 replies
1144 retweets
2271 likes

+++++++

"Not sure you actually came out of it that well, JJ," Phil admits.

"Look, I told Arlo that a bit of beef between me and the young upstart might help the paper. The entrée was today." JJ searches for another morsel of food in the overbearing gloom.

"Try and make sure you win round two, whenever that may be," Phil concedes.

"Look Phil, I'm a wordsmith, right? Storytelling should be a competitive sport. It used to be in my house – that'll be the Irish in us. Every situation when I was growing up was all about the interaction. Everything seemed like a one-act-play. Words are important. I mean, why use one or two words when twenty will do just as well. That's why I hate this twitter malarkey. You can't express yourself properly. It's like asking Michaelangelo to paint the spare fucking bedroom," JJ spits.

Other diners go silent and heads turn in the murk. Phil breaches the gap with a whisper.

"Then don't use twitter. Or any social media, for that matter. Don't try and play him at his game. Use long form to win the war."

JJ doesn't respond. He is staring at nothing in particular. He leans in towards Phil, voice checked.

"You know, in the Wizard of Oz, towards the end, there's a big booming voice that comes out from behind the curtain......."BLAH, BLAH, BLAH." It has gravitas and people believe what he is saying. That's until the moment when the curtain is pulled back by that fucking annoying dog, what's it called.......Toto...... and you see who actually is behind the vocal delivery. The origins of which come from a much smaller man, a less impressive man."

"I remember. It was on TV every Christmas," Phil nods.

"I am that man. I shout, I regale, I judge, I disparage, I belittle. Loudly. Don't get me wrong, all with humour and a deal of fine writing, of course. But, the point is, readers believe me. They hang off my every word."

"Yes, they do."

"I can make or break a restaurant. Or at least I used to be able to. And you know what?"

"What?"

"I hate myself for it."

"Why hate yourself, JJ, why?"

"Because sometimes it's easier to want the attention and admiration of thousands of complete fucking strangers than it is to accept the love and loyalty of those closest to me. I heard that in a song once," JJ confesses. He fastens his eyes firmly on Phil. "And sometimes I prefer to look at myself through someone else's eyes. Eyes that aren't shrouded by knowing what a complete goose I can be."

I feel his tears accumulate. I also feel his relief that the room is in near darkness.

====//====

Why can't I leave Maddy? Is it an admission of failure, a failure to give solace to her just when she needed it most? I can't find the way in to give it to her anyway. If I were leaving for another woman, I would merely be betraying our wedding vows. But to leave Maddy and the girls to be by myself, then surely that's a rejection of everything I hold dear about family. What about my father? Would I be a hypocrite? I think I need to see somebody about this.

====//====

"Gastro confessional."

"What are you on about?"

"This place. The darkness. You can't see the other person. They can't see you. It's like going to confession. Stick that in your Dictaphone. Fuck the food. That almost doesn't matter. I've never known a place that heightens the senses so much and makes you drop your guard all at once. Keep recording, Phil."

Phil fumbles around in his pocket for the recording device. "You rolling?"

"Wait a sec." He depresses a button and says, "I'm guessing that's the right button."

JJ emits a low rumble.

"Nubilus. The art of the kitchen confessional. Never before has a restaurant's ambiance pricked my soul so much. Tastes are heightened to such an extent that they mess with your emotions. Don't worry, Phil, I'll edit this when I get home. I'm guessing that tastes are heightened, Phil? Anyway, where was I? Emotions, emotions, oh yes, mess with your emotions so much, you'll want to confess to a dozen cold case murders or, much worse, tell your wife how you feel. After this rollercoaster of confessional dining in the dark, it wasn't solitude I was feeling, it was more like the worst type of loneliness. Was it the loneliness of being misunderstood or, more likely, the loneliness of being afraid to allow myself to be understood? Yes, I have a confession. Nubilus is a revelation. I must have been blind not to have known this place before now. Full stop. Now turn the fucker off."

"Roger that."

Much louder now, JJ asks nobody in particular.

"Do you think there are lights in the toilet?"

====//====

I penetrate JJ's dream again tonight. He is sat at a rotating conveyor belt which delivers sushi and sashimi to him. Some of the plates contain food that is still alive. Every plate he has his eye on is being snapped up by one of the numerous people hovering to his right. He is getting increasingly agitated. He tries to move seats but he remains exactly where he is. Firstly, he is physically stuck to the seat, like a giant magnet sucking his buttock cheeks into the stool. Next, when he finally manages to stand up, there are no spare seats available. Finally, one appears and JJ races to it, only to find that the chairs are now the conveyor belt and he ends up exactly in the position he started. It seems that anybody to his left now only has half a face, a Daliesque molten clock face dripping onto the floor.

I summon Ella. Again, I try to visualize her fully formed. Her face could never be described as gorgeous or significant, yet I was always drawn to her subdued features, exposed by her unceasing lack of makeup. Maybe she reminded me of Maddy in some way, a way that hinted at better days, happier times. Ella appears, left of dream. I see her plucking dishes one by one from the carousel and resting them on a groaning tray. JJ is still visibly agitated and he is yet to see Ella. He is attempting to push one of the half-faced figures from his stool. Just as one hits the floor, another appears to replace the fallen incumbent. JJ turns, sees the waitress and turns back again to his game of stool skittles. The double-take happens within a second. He turns back to face a welcoming Ella. She offers the tray of goodies to JJ. She smiles, an unmistakably Ella smile. *That's my girl.* JJ is transfixed, agitation diminishing by the moment, drowning in her big, hazel eyes. The more food she affords, the more he visibly relaxes, until he mouths, eyes only for her, "I can taste again."

That should do it. I pull away and let JJ finish whatever dream he wants to dream, safe in the knowledge that another new memory will be created tonight. Ella, both eye candy and soul food.

====//====

Wednesday – Food for Thought – Carnegie Walk, Melbourne

[An immersive interactive dinner performance where your meal is the ultimate three-act drama and where true gastronomy resembles a vibrant symphony for the senses]

I remember back to when JJ opened his writing brief and those three words jumped off the page. Food for Thought. I can only hope and pray that Ella still works there and that she will be working a shift tonight. The thought that she won't be the next part of my journey is too painful to contemplate and I while away the hours of the journey to Melbourne traipsing around the landscape inside JJ's head. In particular, I go looking for signs of Ella.

====//====

As we cross Food for Thought's threshold, whilst JJ is not focusing on anything in particular, my gaze leaps around indiscriminately, searching for Ella. We arrive early for the 7.30 performance – "please remember this is a 3-Act-Performance, not merely a booking, Mr Lowe," the Maitre-D remarks haughtily as he leads us to our table. He puts down two programmes and moves away to greet more guests. All of the tables form a giant semi-circle with what looks like a large light installation taking centre stage. JJ and Phil take their seats and semi-face each other at forty-five degrees, like some kind of business class seating arrangement. JJ is facing away from the waiters and waitresses mingling in the shadows directly behind us. There's no chance of spotting Ella for the moment. I will need to be patient. Besides, JJ is thumbing through the programme of events, his gaze very much front and centre.

"An evening about greatness. Parables and fables," JJ mutters.

"We've had two great nights so far. Fingers crossed for more greatness tonight," Phil responds.

A waitress appears, offering "harvested rainwater."

"If you must," JJ grunts, as the waitress-who-is-not-Ella fills two glasses, positioned in holes at the perimeter of the table, and departs. JJ takes a sip and turns to Phil.

"You know I'm not a big fan of going to the doctors surgery. It normally means that something is amiss in this temple of mine."

"And there's plenty wrong with you, my friend," Phil interrupts.

"But my point is, there is always, and I mean always, an interminable wait to be seen. What do you guys do in there? I would have thought that you'd want to get rid of every ill fucker you see. But no, every appointment goes over time. It got me thinking. People should at least try and learn something when they go to the quacks. There's a pile of magazines there – Nat Geo, New Scientist.......even the Accidental Gourmet, especially when I'm in it. Learn. Inject your life with knowledge. Don't waste your time, especially if you're running out of it."

The place is filling up and there are a couple of spare tables waiting for latecomers. The lights dim.

"Let the show begin," JJ says a little too loudly.

The lights dim further, revealing an adumbral scene and a gentle piano caresses the room. It is joined by a haunting guitar, filling the space further. Eyes focus in on the light installation, as it flashes up the words......

Greatness carries its own penalties

......and then......

The Rose & the Amaranth – Paul Otteson

......now the spectral voice kicks in.......

Neighbour, smile, the sun shines
For it sees in you a splendour
Fairest skin, eyes so blue
The sky demands you tell your secret
Whisper softly to the wind
You must always feel the envy of your friends
And your Mother, is she beautiful?

You are kind, but know the sun shines
Far beyond my brief allure
You've the gift, words so true
Carved upon the stone
They will live on forever
You must know by now, with greatness comes a toll
Ask my Mother, she was beautiful.

The song lasts for a little over two minutes. Lights flash and where once were the song lyrics are now, once again, the words.....

Greatness carries its own penalties

......which suddenly morphs into.......

Greatness in food is the best form of magic

JJ looks down to where food has magically appeared on the table. There is a collective gasp from around the room as diners become aware of what has happened. There is a spontaneous round of applause and diners look at each other and smile. We are less than five minutes in and the atmosphere is already one of collective frivolity and anticipation.

"I'm confused. That wasn't there when we sat down," Phil looks on in awe.

"There's a false top to the table, look." JJ traces the indentation where the inner table has risen, replacing the old top.

Amongst the furore, an aperitif is delivered to the table by another not-Ella-waitress. My internal eye begins darting around again. Still no sign. I need a Plan B, just in case she's a no-show.

Phil reveals a card which is propped up against one of the three dishes on the table. He coughs theatrically and reads from it.

"Entrees. Hiramasa kingfish chowder. Ox neck fricassee. Jerusalem artichoke gratin. Very nice indeed. How are your buds, old buddy?"

"Funny you should ask, but I think they're on the mend. I woke up this morning a little, how can I say, revitalised," JJ responds through a mouthful of chowder.

"Then I can unburden myself from all the pressure of being your chief taster. That's a relief. For the record, this is good," Phil is pointing at the ox neck dish with his fork. He swallows and goes on.

"Roly has been here, you know? He wrote a glowing review. I happen to have a copy of it, for reference purposes only of course, in my pocket."

"Don't mention that name," JJ snaps and forces a fork-full of gratin into his mouth. In amongst some hearty chewing, he adds. "What overblown shit did he spout about this joint, then?"

Phil is already unfolding the guilty article and says, "Thought you wouldn't resist." He continues after a sip of water.

"And I quote........*The nourishing narrative at Food for Thought is art for all five senses, maybe the greatest show in town*........let me skip a bit......listen to this.........*But this is no gastro gimmick, the food gets a five-star review too, local, organic and a dash of the indigenous (no real surprise when one of the founders is an anthropologist), leaving me wallowing in gourmet gemutlichkeit. Ahh, those four words. Heart. Mind. Temper. Feeling. Quite the quartet to get right.......*

Phil looks up, "Do you want me to go on?"

"No thank you, I'm feeling nauseous enough already. Gemutlichkeit? Really?"

"He's got a point, though," Phil counters.

"I'll give you a fucking fable. The ass, the cock and the lion. Heard of it? Very apt after listening to that bollocks."

"Go on," Phil cajoles.

"False confidence often leads to disaster. It's your classic story of A, B and C."

"This'll be good."

"A shouts, real loud. B flees from the sound of A. B seems scared. C then chases after B, thinking he is superior. There's your false confidence. Then guess what happens?" JJ pauses.

"I think I can guess."

"B fucking well eats C, doesn't he? Do not piss around with B. Or you get savaged. Simple as."

"I see."

"Now that's gemutlichkeit."

====//====

The book club came to a rather abrupt end. The first rule about book club is... you don't talk about book club. Well, not in a disparaging way, anyway. When the word on the street was that it was a drinking group with a reading problem, it was probably time to call it a day. Especially, when the word on the street was perpetrated by its own members. Plus, there are only so many books you can read about terminal illness, memory loss or apocalyptic dawns before you want to chuck yourself under a bus or, at the very least, leave the 500-page door-stop untouched on the bedside table.

All of this helped to drag things closer to the edge, but the actual tipping point came when Pablo chose a book written by a local author. There was nothing wrong per se in that, after all the novel had garnered decent enough reviews in the Sunday supplements. It was when he invited the author, secretly, to attend our monthly rendezvous, only for none of the group (bar Pablo, of course) to have actually read the said tome, that the first rule became the worst rule. The worst rule about book club is... you don't talk about book club... not even amongst your members.

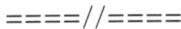

"Since when did the world change, Phil?" JJ returns from practicing his lines in the bathroom. He rubs his nose and continues without waiting for an answer.

"I always thought that the answers, whatever they were, would be found be society as a whole or in your community or family, but now..." he trails off for a second then remounts the horse, "but now, you have to search deep inside yourself for answers, like we're the only fuckers that can help ourselves."

"Ahh, the rise of the self-help book," Phil butts in.

"Exactly! And don't get me started on Wii Fit and the Atkins Diet. We can't be expected to find all the answers ourselves, whatever the answer is it must exist in others."

"As a doctor, what annoys me most are, on the one hand, those who come in and tell me, the professional," Phil's index fingers form quotation marks for effect, "what exactly is wrong with them. And then there are those who you help but they are completely unable to help themselves when they leave the clinic."

"I think that I fall into both those camps!" JJ hoots, sniffing wildly.

"Sometimes all within the one appointment!" Phil howls.

"Well, I've decided that I'm going to help myself from now on. I write but I don't deal in truths. And that's another reason why I hate myself," JJ throws his napkin onto the table.

"I'm not sure I follow. You do speak the truth in your reviews, don't you?"

"Maybe a pseudo truth or an embellished one, perhaps. But I am just one person, who has one very tired voice. Even the wanker from Warsaw believes that. It's the other voices I need to find. The others."

"Now you're really speaking in tongues."

"I want to write a novel. There I've said it. You see, a novelist is not one person, he is free to inhabit others and as a writer, do you know how fucking liberating that is?" The couple behind Phil turn and glower in our direction. JJ continues his diatribe.

"You can not just be what you know, but all the things you don't know too. Stories in the guise of lies poison our world, Phil, but stories as fiction, well they can transform and transcend because they contain truths, not lies. Truths from the others. Stories of people, of other people, remind us that we are not alone and that, my friend, is the power of the novel."

"JJ, I think you should see a shrink."

====//====

I went through a European book phase where Kafka and Satre rubbed existential shoulders with Tolstoy and Nabokov, but my favourite was Milan Kundera. I loved his writing. Damn, I even wanted to be him. My diary entries even started to take on a new style.

====//====

Thursday 11th December

Thought for the day. If we only have one life to live, we might as well have not lived at all. I crave this kind of lightness. I want to be light, not like Maddy, weighed down by the world. I thought that we built our foundations on higher ground. The problem is, the higher you are, the colder it can get.

Sunday 21st January

Hot one today. Took the girls to the cemetery on the hill to see my grandfather's grave. How less rich this world would be without its graves, without the memories of those long gone. Only those without a voice speak forever.

====//====

A bright spotlight shines through the screen. Black vertical bars appear, behind which the shadow of a model sits. Maudlin strings caress the air and a voice declares the start of Act II. The room is hushed and the voice continues.

Excerpts from A Hunger Artist – Franz Kafka (translation by W & E Muir)

"*During these last decades the interest in professional fasting has markedly diminished. It used to pay very well to stage such great performances under one's own management, but today that is quite impossible. We live in a different world now. At one time the whole town took a lively interest in the hunger artist......*"

More shadows materialize and congregate around the cage. The narrator continues.

"*From day to day of his fast the excitement mounted; everybody wanted to see him at least once a day; there were people who bought season tickets for the last few days and sat from morning till night in front of his small barred cage; even in the night time there were visiting hours, when the whole effect was heightened by torch flares........*"

JJ's eyes dart around the spectacle but I am fixed on one shadow in particular. How can you tell one shadow from another? Surely, they are all pretty much the same, right? Except maybe large or small, thick or thin. This shadow is different, for this particular shadow has Maddy's nose. And that can only mean one thing.

"On fine days the cage was set out in the open air, and then it was the children's special treat to see the hunger artist; for their elders he was often just a joke that happened to be in fashion, but the children stood open-mouthed, holding each other's hands for greater security, marvelling at him as he sat there pallid in black tights, with his ribs sticking out so prominently, not even on a seat but down among straw on the ground, sometimes giving a courteous nod, answering questions with a constrained smile, or perhaps stretching an arm through the bars so that one might feel how thin it was, and then again withdrawing deep into himself, paying no attention to anyone or anything, not even to the all-important striking of the clock that was the only piece of furniture in his cage, but merely staring into vacancy with half-shut eyes, now and then taking a sip from a tiny glass of water to moisten his lips."

JJ mirrors the narrative and takes a sip from his water. Maybe it is the new inner novelist in him, but he seems transfixed by the performance. I am transfixed by the nose. It is one of those convex noses, the type that curves outwards in the central area and protrudes a little too far from the face. Perfect for a strong outline in the shadows. Overprojected. Yes, that's what it is. And so Maddy. She told me off once when I called it a Roman nose. *No, no, no, it's actually an Aquiline nose*, she said. Michael once remarked, and got away with it, that she could smoke in the shower. Surely, Ella had one too. Think, think, think, man.

"The longest period of fasting was fixed by his impresario at forty days, beyond that term he was not allowed to go, not even in great cities, and there was good reason for it, too. Experience had proved that for about forty days the interest of the public could be stimulated by a steadily increasing pressure of advertisement, but after that the town began to lose interest and sympathetic support began notably to fall off. So on the fortieth day the flower-bedecked cage was opened, enthusiastic spectators filled the hall, a military band played, two doctors entered the cage to measure the results of the fast, which were announced through a megaphone, and finally two young ladies appeared, blissful at having been selected for the honour, to help the hunger artist down the few steps leading to a small table on which was spread a carefully chosen invalid repast."

JJ mimics the intonation as he leans sideways towards Phil.

"Invalid repast. I've had a few of those in my time." Phil ignores him, eyes fused to the show of shadows. The narrator continues apace.

"So he lived for many years, with small regular intervals of recuperation, in visible glory, honoured by all the world, yet in spite of that troubled in spirit, and all the more troubled because no one would take his trouble seriously. A few years later when the witnesses of such scenes called them to mind, they often failed to understand themselves at all. For meanwhile, a change in public interest had set in; it seemed to happen almost overnight; there

may have been profound causes for it, but who was going to bother about that; at any rate the pampered hunger artist suddenly found himself deserted one fine day by the amusement seekers, who went streaming past him to other more favoured attractions. Fasting would surely come into fashion again at some future date, yet that was no comfort for those living in the present. What, then, was the hunger artist to do? He had been applauded by thousands in his time and could hardly come down to showing himself in a street booth at village fairs, and as for adopting another profession, he was not only too old for that but too fanatically devoted to fasting. So he took leave of the impresario, his partner in an unparalleled career, and hired himself to a large circus; in order to spare his own feelings he avoided reading the conditions of his contract."

"Schoolboy error. Always read the contract, buddy. They always try and screw you over," JJ whispers to nobody in particular.

"He took it as a matter of course that he and his cage should be stationed, not in the middle of the ring as a main attraction, but outside, near the animal cages, on a site that was after all easily accessible. When the first great rush was past, the stragglers came along, and these, whom nothing could have prevented from stopping to look at him as long as they had breath, raced past with long strides, hardly even glancing at him, in their haste to get to the menagerie in time. Perhaps, said the hunger artist to himself many a time, things could be a little better if his cage were set not quite so near the menagerie. But he did not dare to lodge a

complaint with the management; after all, he had the animals to thank for the troops of people who passed his cage, among whom there might always be one here and there to take an interest in him. He might fast as much as he could, and he did so; but nothing could save him now, people passed him by. Just try to explain to anyone the art of fasting!"

"Not sure I understand why, my friend," JJ answers. "Can't see the point. Maybe there's a truth in there somewhere." The shadow theatre is now shrouded briefly in black. When the light materialises again, the cage is empty.

Many more days went by, however, and that too came to an end. An overseer's eye fell on the cage one day and he asked the attendants why this perfectly good cage should be left standing there unused with dirty straw inside it; nobody knew, until one man, helped out by the notice board, remembered about the hunger artist. They poked into the straw with sticks and found him in it. "Are you still fasting?" asked the overseer, "when on earth do you mean to stop?" "Forgive me, everybody," whispered the hunger artist, only the overseer, who had his ear to the bars, understood him. "Of course," said the overseer, and tapped his forehead with a finger to let the attendants know what state the man was in, "we forgive you." "I always wanted you to admire my fasting," said the hunger artist. "We do admire it," said the overseer, affably. "But you shouldn't admire it," said the hunger artist. "Well then we don't admire it," said the overseer, "but why shouldn't we admire it?" "Because I have to fast, I can't help it," said the hunger artist.

"What a fellow you are," said the overseer, "and why can't you help it?" "Because," said the hunger artist, lifting his head a little and speaking, with his lips pursed, as if for a kiss, right into the overseer's ear, so that no syllable might be lost, "because I couldn't find the food I liked. If I had found it, believe me, I should have made no fuss and stuffed myself like you or anyone else." These were his last words, but in his dimming eyes remained the firm though no longer proud persuasion that he was continuing to fast.

JJ swallows. It's time to prick the Ella balloon. I sprint back into the bank of memories. Luckily, I don't have to travel far - the 'new' section is close by. And there is the hook-nosed, sushi waitress I am looking for, handing out morsels for our smitten hero. I poke and jostle, arousing the memory further. I head back, hoping for Ella to appear in real life for JJ.

"Well, clear this out now!" said the overseer, and they buried the hunger artist, straw and all. Into the cage they put a young panther. Even the most insensitive felt it refreshing to see this wild creature leaping around the cage that had so long been dreary. The panther was all right. The food he liked was brought him without hesitation by the attendants; he seemed not even to miss his freedom; his noble body, furnished almost to the bursting point with all that it needed, seemed to carry freedom around with it too; somewhere in his jaws it seemed to lurk; and the joy of life streamed with such ardent passion from his throat that for the on-lookers it was not easy to stand the shock of it. But they braced

themselves, crowded round the cage, and did not want ever to move away."

The strings start up again and a quote appears out of the light box, suspending itself in mid-air, almost touchable..........

Do not confuse notoriety and fame with greatness. For you see, greatness is a measure of one's spirit and not a result of one's rank in human affairs – Sherman Finesilver

There is a smattering of applause around the room and a couple of the diners attempt to touch the words dangling in front of them. The ambient light is returned to the dining space. Phil turns to JJ and raises a solitary eyebrow.

"You can read my mind, Phillip."

"Am I right, then?"

"You tell me. So what am I thinking?"

"That this is, how would you say it, a load of bollocks? Or is it a manifestation of truths? I'm not sure what you're think-ing anymore," Phil chuckles.

"Neither do I at the moment. It's strange, but *that* reminds me of a woman. A woman I used to know. At least, I think I used to know her."

Know her? I just need you to recognize her.

====//====

By day, I wade through the irksome banalities of married life. By night, I am in bed, floating in a sea of emerald. Saying goodnight, Maddy hovers over me, trespassing, a wave tainting my flesh. We collide and her colours ravage me. And there is nothing I can do about it. My dreams are getting increasingly more sinister.

But there is this collision of conscience, this conflict of the mind. There is beauty in humdrum despite few memories being innate there. Then reality bites. All the things I want to escape from are exactly the things that plenitude will come from. Embracing the mundane means ditching the pursuit of the extraordinary. Damn this collision. No, it is merely two sides of the same coin, we need the banality so that we can escape into the fantastical, and neither can exist without the other.

From eternity to here. If I can't live with her, maybe I can live within her.

====//====

"Unravelling external selves and coming home to our real identity is the true meaning of soul work." – Sue Monk Kidd

I sense the exact moment he sees her. Of course, I spotted her first. Phil is talking about a recent holiday with Judy and JJ has just deposited a forkful of moist sea bream into his mouth. He stares, tracking her slowly from table to table and then to the point where she disappears behind a curtain heading for the kitchen housed behind it.

"......it was quite remarkable," Phil says. And then, "JJ, are you alright? You look like you've seen a ghost."

"I, err, I have to go and check something out. Would you mind? I'm terribly, err, sorry," is all JJ can offer. Phil shakes his head.

"I don't think I've ever heard you apologise for anything. Actually, apart from the inescapable *I'm sorry if I've offended you*." But JJ is not listening. He is following the scent of his dream woman, also known as my ticket home.

Everything moves in slow motion. JJ shuffles across the room towards his vision. Finally, he stands within touching distance of her. It is definitely her. One hundred percent. Touching distance. She is facing a computer screen.

After what seems like an age, JJ asks. "Do I know you from somewhere?"

Ella shakes her head and says simply, "I don't think so." She continues touch-typing on the screen.

"I'm sure I do."

She looks up, shakes her head and returns to the screen.

"I'm sure you don't," one of Ella's fellow waitresses butts in.

JJ presses on, "I think I dreamt of you last night."

"Ewww," the other waitress decries.

"It may sound weird but it's true. I have been dreaming of you."

Oh God, that sounds worse.

"Listen up, you creep. Leave Ella alone or I'll be forced to call management."

Shit. Not good. Not good at all.

"But.....but.....I'm not a creep. I'm.....I'm serious. She was like Wonder Woman in one and then like, I don't know, Wonder Waitress in another," garbles JJ. He is seriously flustered.

"I mean it, I'm calling management," says the other waitress, disappearing behind the curtain. Ella just stands there, remarkably composed.

Holy crap, this is not going well.

"Please. Please believe me," JJ desperately says to Ella. His tone is calmer, more insistent even. "I'm sorry if I'm creeping you out. You have to believe me. OK, I'll leave you alone now."

"Wonder Woman?" Ella smiles for the first time. Maddy's smile. I smile back.

There is a commotion behind Ella.

"Yes, my Wonder Woman." JJ reaches out, takes Ella's hand and kisses it.

Bang! I am gone! The ride is smoother this time, familiar even. I am such an old pro at this now. One more to go. One more.

I see the words *I'm sorry* form on JJ's lips as he is led away by two hefty blokes, the thin slice of ham between two huge doorstop slices of bread. I see Phil's look of bewilderment from across the room. I see other diners one-by-one turn their heads to witness the clamour. I see what Ella sees. I see home.

====//====

I remember hearing something interesting when listening with Ned to a radio documentary. It talked of how music can detonate a sense of yearning. It is called tizita, meaning nostalgia, longing or memory. There are some songs which draw on memories of lost loves, childhood or, simply, home.

You know it's nearly Christmas when you hear Paul Kelly's *How to Make Gravy* on the radio. That is my tizita. I miss my home. I listen to the words with fresh ears. It is sung by a man stuck in prison, desperate to be home for Christmas. How apt. I know Joe in the song doesn't make it. My tizita longs that I do.

Ella is sat at her kitchen counter, making Christmas paraphernalia. Ella is obviously a bit like Maddy when it comes to the idea of a gift. I was always a let's-get-in-and-out-of-town-in-an-hour kind of guy when it came to Christmas shopping. I hated it, but still went in for the materialistic store-based treasure hunt scrimmage. Maddy, on the other hand, was much more practical and was in her element making, yes actually making, presents for people. She would manufacture jars of chutney, preserved fruits and pickled vegetables, an assembly line of festive waste-not-want-not. All with personalized labels too. Quite the domestic goddess.

Ella takes a 2-litre plastic bottle from the recycling bin and cuts the top off it in a rather imprecise way. She wanders over to her drinks cabinet and appropriates a bottle of Swedish vodka. She then sits the vodka bottle inside the plastic container. She has assembled a pile of berries, herbs, holly leaves, zest and slices from oranges and lemons on the worktop and starts to shove them down the sides. She fills the plastic sleeve up with water from the tap, suspending the contents in a watery prison. Opening the freezer drawer, she slides in the bottles, keeping them upright, a satisfied Christmassy beam on her face.

Now it's time for her to get creative with crackers. It is a shame that it won't be me pulling one this year. I also begin to worry that she is in the process of trying to inherit the make-and-make-do tiara from Maddy. Is this hitherto unseen trait from Ella telling me something, or am I being paranoid?

I have been scratching the surface of Ella's short-term memories, hoping for fresh clues about what happened. There is no time or date stamp so it is hard to fathom whether a memory of Ella and Maddy is pre or post the accident. Memories have immense staying power but most tend to thrive in the dark, surviving for decades even in the deep waters of our minds, like shipwrecks lying on the seabed. Maybe the most recent memories haven't had enough time to sink to the bottom yet. It is dreams that linger nearer the surface, our dreams that help keep us afloat, rather than our memories which weigh us down.

Ella notices the answer phone flashing and drops the two cardboard toilet roll centres she is attempting to weld together to make the barrel of the cracker. She depresses the play button and I hear my brother's voice at the end of the phone line.

- Hi, L, it's me Mikey. You going to pick up?

There's a pause, then Michael's voice again.

- Maybe not. Anyway, suppose I'll catch you later at the hospital. Don't forget to bring Mad and the girls' presents. See ya.

Maddy's alive! Maddy's alive! And my girls! I will see them again. Paranoia over.

====//====

I wonder if people will believe that there is a curse attached to me or my family. Losing a child confronts our understanding of fairness, that your life exists in some kind of good-bad equilibrium. Then comes the horror crash, the second serving of calamity to hit the family. And the talk of a curse follows.

If Maddy blamed herself for one tragedy, she will undoubtedly do it again for mine. She obviously wants to be culpable in an ordered world, a world where people are punished arbitrarily for something they have or haven't done. I prefer the other school of thought. Curses are hokum. Whatever happens, we are all blameless and adrift in the random squalls of the cosmos. When I get back, I will tell her that. Just to dulcify her broken heart.

Ella is a soft talker, so soft that people sometimes find her hard to understand. Sentences trail off into nothingness, as though she has changed her mind halfway or, more likely, her mind has moved on to other priorities. Do not confuse this with her having nothing to say. She is fiercely bright and, I hate to say it, puts Maddy somewhat in the shade with her intellect.

====//====

The intercom buzzes impatiently and Ella rises to answer it. It is Rob, her on/off boyfriend, who obviously is more on than off at the present time. I have met Rob a few times and he seems a decent bloke. He claims to be an activist but isn't much active in anything, apart from complaining and being cynical about almost everything. He is a paid up member of the "all-mouth-and-no-trousers" brigade, which Ella outwardly despises, hence my surprise that their relationship seems to be 'in the black' again.

Ella firmly believes in the possibility of the world living in a state of utopia. I remember long arguments with her about it, why I thought she needed to open her eyes to the real world, her insistence that the good side of human nature will out, if given the chance.

"Are you ready for your present?" Ella asks, unscrewing two bottles of beer. She hands one to Rob, who is lounging on a beanbag in the centre of the room.

"I thought we weren't doing, you know, gifts this year," Rob stammers, clearly in a state of panic.

"Well, we weren't but I saw this in the Op shop," she holds the beautifully wrapped gift aloft, "and I thought of you, actually us." Ella throws the rectangle to Rob, who snares it with aplomb.

"Can I open it now, or wait for tomorrow?"

"Now, you fool. Let's call it our Christmas Eve entertainment. Anything's better than carols on the box."

Rob slides his finger gently under the taped flap.

"Do you want to keep the paper?"

"No, don't worry. Go for your life!"

Rob tears at the printed green reindeers in mock mania and unveils a board game which has seen better days.

"What the...? Gaz-dal-kodj Oko-san," he struggles to read the name printed on the front. I recognize the game, though.

"Cool, huh? It's Hungarian. It's a socialist version of Monopoly from their Iron Curtain days." Ella adds, smugly.

"Love it, El. Love *it*," Rob emphasizes the last 'it'.

"Shall we get down to it, then?" Ella says seductively.

"Ooh, yes, comrade," breathes Rob, unpacking the board and the contents of the box.

Ella throws a large cushion on the floor opposite Rob and reads from the instruction sheet (luckily, there's an English section). She takes a swig from her beer and begins.

"Blah, blah, blah, ahh, here we go. The aim of the game is not to amass an empire of property or wealth. It is to save enough to buy an apartment and subsequently fully furnish it."

"Oh, I'm loving this," Rob butts in, "look, there are spaces for the zoo, the butcher, the shoe shop, the liquour store. And the tobacco shop!" Rob squeals with delight.

"OK. The 'GO' square is the factory and every time you land on it or pass it, it is payday. Once you have saved enough, you can buy an apartment, or make a down-payment, blah, blah, have the balance deducted from your weekly paycheck."

"Oh, this is gold, El," Rob bellows.

"Once you have fully purchased your apartment, you can buy kitchen and bathroom furniture from the store on square 14," Ella points to the salient square on the faded board. She goes on, "you can also get appliances, like a radio, a washing machine, a sewing machine, yeah, from the store on square 30."

"What's the 'Wheel of Fortune'? " Rob asks.

"I guess we'll find out. Oh, listen to this. Your wage is your income, and that is fixed. You are not to make profit off your proletarian neighbours, at any cost. Players may not sell property or furniture to each other."

"Wow, no wonder the black markets thrived in these places," Rob sniggers.

"Shall we start? You can be the hammer and I'll be the sickle."

"You should be the furry hat. Very Doctor Zhivago."

"Let's roll."

Whilst this is an endearing scene, I decide to retreat and let the lovebirds get on with their parade through the fiscal minefield of a planned economy in a 40 year-old board game. I recede into Ella's memory bank, searching again for clues from the accident. I decussate access points to potential recollections, but these memories are like mercury. Each time I get close, they disperse, slipping out of my fingers like a bar of soap. Then one persists, too sluggish to resist my grasp. I recognize instantly the protagonists. Maddy is there, puffy-eyed, sapped, somehow drawn, yet still beautiful. Ella's apartment, sun pouring through the half-open blinds, the trace of freshly roasted coffee permeating the scene..."it's all my fault"..."I'm not good enough for him"...over and over through the tears. Again and again. I disengage, numb, thinking of an old diary entry.

====//====

Thursday 23rd May

Love is. There used to be a cartoon strip called that in the newspaper when I was a kid. Love is being able to say you're sorry, and all that type of thing. They never said that love is about weakness, being touched by another's frailties and sorrows. Seeing

Maddy in crisis reassures me that she is not invincible. Me supporting her will reduce my sense of inadequacy, surely. We could even share the pain together. If she'd ever let me.

====//====

"Payday!" Rob rubs his hands as he passes GO again, adding, "I reckon I can afford a down payment soon. My own little commie apartment."

"This game has some merits," Ella says in her soft voice.

"Why so?"

"I've already talked to you about the universal basic wage, haven't I?"

"Ahh, your utopian dream. It'll never catch on, El."

"Just makes sense to me. Everyone gets paid, and I mean everyone, a basic wage so they can afford stuff, like better food, housing, you know, the stuff that makes life more tolerable."

"Drugs, man," Rob giggles. Ella stays serious, her voice not as soft as before.

"They've done trials and it really works. Healthcare costs go down because people are living above the poverty line. Poverty just means no money. It doesn't have to mean no hope."

"So, just give everybody money and it solves everything? Who pays for it?" Rob enquires.

"I've told you before! It pays for itself in healthcare costs. There's no strain on the system and people can choose to do more self-fulfilling jobs or even job share because of the basic wage. Everyone feels better about themselves."

"There's always shit jobs that need doing."

"I know, but we might get rid of a few jobs that provide, well, literally nothing to society."

"Like what?"

"I dunno. PR people, I guess. What about food critics. I mean, what does a food critic contribute to society anyway." Ella smiles, lightening the mood. Rob beams in return. As do I, although I can think of one food critic that has made a telling contribution in my society. Ella throws a three and moves to the Wheel of Fortune square. Rob picks up a card from the middle and reads.

"Exercise is healthy and entertaining. Move to space 11. Oh no, I picked up two cards. They were stuck together. I'll put that one back, here's yours. HA! You have dirtied the street. Pay 10 florints!" Rob laughs and coughs at the same time, spluttering, "no new vacuum cleaner for you, comrade."

"It doesn't say that!" Ella protests. Rob shows her the card, still laughing.

"I love this game!"

With Ella going backwards a few trips around the board in her pursuit of buying and furnishing a flat, I detach myself from the game and go exploring again.

====//====

It's Christmas morning and Ella wakes to the display of shafts of sunlight dancing across the bed. They have reached the latitude of her pillow, inducing her eyes open to celebrate their merry jig. It is a solitary scene, as only I share the yuletide panorama with Ella, Rob having been kicked out around midnight after winning the excruciatingly long game of 'Commiopoly' (as they penned it). Today is the day that I return home, seeing Maddy and my girls for the first time in nearly three months.

Ella stands completely naked in front of the full-length mirror, eyeing herself up and down, no doubt contemplating some silent feedback. I recoil into the darkness, wearing the guilty cloak of the unintentional voyeur. I contemplate what it would be like cocooned inside Maddy, the woman I once wanted to spend the rest of my life with. Rather perversely, I am looking forward to spending the rest of my death with her. Now, second thoughts begin to engulf me suddenly. I even wonder whether it would be possible to inhabit an object, rather than a subject. Maybe an armchair or the chest of drawers, always there, diligently watching over the comings and goings of her life. I think of the salt and pepper pots from Beauty and the Beast and all of the Toy Story toys and wouldn't it be better to observe, rather than feel, Maddy's life without me? No, I want to allay fears and make peace, to temper the grief and nurture hope. I need to. I also need to hope that Ella has got some clothes on by the time I resurface.

====//====

Carols radiate from the radio on the kitchen window ledge, as Ella brews coffee on the stove top. I have always liked Ella. She has been a constant when it came to me and Maddy, both in our rise and our fall. A willing accomplice in the rise and a perpetual thorn in preventing the fall.

What of my memories? My body was the only thing I had to say goodbye to. I seem to have held on to my memories, and in that lies a comfort. They are moveable objects, never set in stone. They may have become lost, but they can easily be refound, reignited, changed or augmented even, by the slightest prick. A sight, a sound or a smell. Or me searching for clues. Sometimes, the richness of our lives lies in the memories we have neglected. I've heard it said that the human soul weighs 21 grams. Maybe that is the sum weight of our memories that we take with us after we are gone. Just as I hope that people do not forget me, my memory cache allows me the same privilege of never forgetting them.

====//====

I must have walked down the road leading to the esplanade a thousand times, maybe more. I have even staggered down here a few times late at night, in my younger years, out of my mind. But I have never walked along here inside the mind of someone else. It somehow looks different when viewed through somebody else's eyes, just like it would feel different walking in another's shoes.

The street seems brighter today, the trees lining the road, practically bursting through the pavement, stretching upwards to the sun; the laneways branching off left and right like multicoloured tendrils; palm trees visible on the horizon as the road pulls us towards the beach. We walk past the old Village Hall, now a modish vegan eaterie, its cream façade in need of a chromatic facelift. There, opposite, is the Gundogumu Turkish café, home of the strongest coffee outside of Istanbul and purveyors of the finest baklava in St. Kilda, or so the sign would have passers-by believe. Through the community gardens, weaving past yuletide picnickers and backyard cricketers. Families enjoying the weather together, families enjoying Christmas together, families just enjoying. Families just being families. And onto the Surf Lifesavers Club, overlooking the wooden boardwalk that skirts the shallow stretch of beach.

Ella bounds up the stairs and enters a room with half a dozen people dotted around a large table. Beads of all colours, elastic chord, cotton thonging and stretch thread are scattered across the table's surface. Maddy had often talked about Ella and her craftivist collective; about how she felt that the world could be changed one stitch at a time; about how the book club, or lack of it at the time, had left a huge hole in her social life; about how Ella was much more worthy than her for doing this; about how she would join next week, no doubt about it; about how she didn't have the time or the energy, what with the girls and all their after-school activities; about how I was stopping her from doing things. The view from Ella's eyes seems brighter than ever, December morning sunlight casting lasers through the surf club windows, notwithstanding. There is a sheen on life I haven't witnessed since Ned. I wonder how the view will feel from inside Maddy, dimmer switch permanently on.

Ella pulls up a chair next to an elderly lady.

"When I came here nearly 60 years ago as a 10-pound-pom, who would have thought that I'd be making bracelets for peace in the Middle East on Christmas Day?!"

"Are you seeing family this Christmas, Alice?" Ella asks.

"Nooo, I'll be seeing them in the New Year."

"Don't you get lonely at this time of year. I always think that Christmas is a time for families to get together."

"Christmas is overrated. I don't believe in Christ or God or whoever. He's a mean spirited bugger if he does exist. That's all I know," Alice suppresses a giggle.

"It's nice to see family though, isn't it?"

Amen to that

"It's nice to see family at any time. It doesn't have to be bloomin' Christmas. Anyway, I see you lot, you know, the Crafty Co-op as my family. I get to see you all much more often and I'm doing some good in the world. Don't need no God to do that," Alice supposes, pulling her beading board closer. It resembles some kind of bagatelle game from my childhood, horseshoe in shape with space for three strands. There are re-cessed wells, already replete with needles, pliers and small ac-cent beads.

"Can I watch?" Ella points to Alice's porcelain fingers hov-ering over the board.

"Of course you can darling. Here goes...beads for Beirut," she cackles, placing a pair of miniature wire cutters next to the board.

"You're a poppet. Talk me through it, I want to learn from the expert," Ella pulls her chair closer. I want her to stand up, walk out, head for the hospital, not to pass GO and collect $200, just go straight to Maddy. Right now. I've waited long enough. But I refrain from shouting my wishes. I want to leave Ella intact, without the burden of voices, of external forces operating internally. Ella will be my virgin hostess, untouched by my demands. I think that only fair. She is family, after all.

"You need to decide how long you want your bracelet and add about 6 inches," Alice cuts a piece of beading wire to her desired length. A wave engulfs me suddenly, throwing me off kilter. I see Alice mouthing something at Ella, but the words that come out are Maddy's.

"In Row 1 of the beading board," Alice points, Maddy continues, "you need to lay out the pattern, like this." Alice overlays the paper pattern on to the board. Maddy continues the lesson.

"Now, centre a bead on the 'O' mark then on either side of it place a jump ring and then another bead. See?" We do. We also hear. It is a memory of Maddy teaching Ella how to make a bracelet. It comes like a tsunami, sucking the present out to sea, replacing it with the deluge of the memory.

"Repeat this pattern until you've got 5 beads either side of the 'O' mark. Then a jump ring, bicone, and another jump ring will see you to within an inch of the length of the finished bracelet. It's that simple," Alice smiles, but all I see is Maddy. She is younger, happier, unbroken and I am flung back into the waves. I let them toss me around for a while, until I am dragged violently under. Gasping for air, I resurface. I am looking straight at a bemused Ella. Alice relinquishes her grip on Ella's hand.

"You look a bit confused, love. Shall I go through it all again, dear?"

Shit. I'm in Alice. This isn't good.

"No, it's OK," Ella gasps, "I'd better be getting off to the hospital soon. I think my sister has been trying to call me," she says, checking her mobile phone for signs of activity. She stands up, putting distance between her and Alice.

Oh, this isn't good at all.

"Have a lovely what's left of Christmas, Alice," Ella remarks. She starts to walk towards the door and says, tailing off, in typical Ella style. "And thanks for the lesson. It, well, rather blew my mind." With that, she walks out of the room, leaving Alice tying overhand knots in the beading wire and me wondering what the hell to do next.

====//====

I remember like it was yesterday. Dad had a swear jar. Mum brought it home one day and called it the "Cussin' Container." Every time anyone swore, they would have to put a dollar into the jar. Of course, Michael and me were too young to swear, in public anyway, and I don't think I had ever heard mum swear. So, it was for dad, really. But the beauty of the cussin' container lay in mum's decision that, at the end of every week, Michael and me would pocket the proceeds, split fifty-fifty to spend how we wished. It started with an accident. Michael was taking a cup of coffee mum had made for dad to him in his study. Spilling some of the coffee on some of dad's papers was, firstly, an obvious accident; secondly, the unfortunate event that donated a couple of gold coins to the swear jar and, most importantly; thirdly, the catalyst for Michael to turn every opportunity for annoying our father into a lucrative business operation.

The endgame was so clear in his young mind – getting dad to swear meant more comics or books or sweets or records. He even took his first girlfriend to the movies on the back of an errant shit or fuck from my potty-mouthed father. Michael was relentless in his pursuit. It stopped when dad moved out. Looking back, I probably need not have blamed myself so much for dad moving out, Michael's "bucks for fucks" strategy played a large part too.

The demise of the swear jar came with an act of sabotage. This time, Michael had nothing to do with it. Mum and dad had some kind of argument over something trivial. We could hear everything start to escalate and it was then that my father told my mother to "F&%k off". She then told him it was "five dollars in the swear jar," to which dad exploded, grabbed the jar and threw it at mum, shouting, "the amount of money

I've put in here could finance the fucking space programme!"
The jar narrowly missed mum and smashed into many pieces
against the wall behind her. I ran immediately to my bedroom.
Michael, on the other hand, waited for the room to clear so he
could collect all the winnings from the floor. Dad moved out
shortly after the incident and the swear jar was no more. The
mark in the wall is still there, though.

====//====

The closer you get to something, the further away it can seem.
Plus ca change, plus c'est la meme chose, and all that. Out of
the frying pan and into the fire. You know the story. I can't see
the woods for the trees and if the finishing line was strung up
between two of them, I'd probably end up garrotting myself. It
feels like I'm making my getaway on a rocking horse.

Things are different in here. There are echoes that reverberate
and I go searching for signs of life, or should I say death. But it
is especially dark in here, not the kind of dark you experience in
the depths of night, but more sinister, a head-turning maze of
cackles and dry ice, a cauldron stirred, a witch's brew of a mind.
I hear voices, but nobody is here. No Jeet to guide me now, just
background noise and a distinct whiff of senescent pot-pourri.
Panic swells. I yell out.

Ella!! Ella!! Come back!!

My cries are swallowed whole and spat out, ripples radiating out in her mind's eye, the same deep water. Alice is one tough nut to crack. How do I alter her delicate circuits that shape her emotions, that react with her memories, that shift her actions, right now? I run headlong into the walls, hoping to trigger some kind of reaction. If she cries out in pain, will Ella come running back? I burst front and centre and practically detonate into her eyeballs.

You MUST find Ella. Pleeeease.

I try to make myself heard, as if positioning myself, arms asunder in a Kate Winslet Titanic pose, is going to fix things. Alice is having none of it and continues threading beads one-by-one, oblivious to my pleas. Precious seconds tick by. She will be out of the building by now, surely, and on her way to seeing and touching, yes, touching Maddy. The light in the room changes imperceptibly and Alice glances up. Ella is looking directly at us, smiling.

"I must be losing my mind. I almost forgot what I came in here for in the first place, Alice," Ella says, matter-of-factly.

"I thought you'd gone for good," Alice replies.

"Will you please make a little necklace for my two nieces?"

"Oh, it'll be my pleasure. You should have said before. Now, come sit down again and choose the colours."

Ella sits within touching distance and I ready myself, lurking in the foretaste of the slightest hint of contact, ripe to move on the 't' of touch. Alice is now restringing the ends and reaches for the crimping pliers. I notice her hands, gnarled like some medieval oak, veins rising, coming up for air. I will them to reach across and touch Ella's hands in some kind of symbolic old-meets-new gesture. It would be more than symbolic for me. It would mean everything. Suddenly, I sense Alice's leg rub up against something. Chutes at the ready, I mobilise in an instant, freefalling, falling, falling...WALLOP...rising, rising, rising again, back to where I started. Alice looks down under the table, the bruise already forming on her leg, the wholly innocent chair leg staring back stubbornly. My thoughts of occupying a chest of drawers in our house to watch over Maddy and the girls have been laid to rest. I cannot transmigrate into solid objects, however much I want to. There will be no plan B, it's Maddy or bust.

And then it happens. Alice trims the excess wire from both ends of the necklace and beckons Ella closer.

"Let me see if this fits," she says, reaching forward meeting Ella halfway. She places the necklace over Ella's head and brushes her ear in doing so..........

Gawwwwwnnnn!

The brightness disorientates me for a second, but I know I am back in Ella. Fearful of another mishap, I bury myself in a corner, my own little panic room. Time passes. I hear muffled conversation, so deep I am trying to hide. I don't even notice Ella get up and leave for a second and, thankfully, final time. What I do notice as we cross the esplanade on the way to the hospital is what the beads on the necklace spell out...

—-[]=**D**=[]=**A**=[]=**D**=[]=**D**=[]=**Y**=[]—-

====//====

Friday 8th October

We go home tomorrow. Holiday has been okay. At least the girls seemed to have enjoyed it. I'm not only going to say it, but I'm going to do it tomorrow. I'm going to leave Maddy. She'll want to tell her girl friends that it's a trial separation, but she can do what she wants because I'm going to do what I want. There's not one person who is going to stop me from leaving her for good. No-one.

====//====

Ella doesn't knock as she enters. The room is dimly lit, but there are unmistakably figures lurking in here. I hear a *Merry Christmas, Ella*, then see Michael rising from a chair.

"Merry Christmas to you too," utters Ella quietly, trying not to disturb the peace enveloping the room. She closes the door in slow motion. The girls run up to her and embrace a leg each. I try to imbibe their love through Ella. Maddy (Oh, Maddy) is slouched in the chair next to the bed. She tries to get up but gets tangled in the wires and tubes emanating from the bedside apparatus. Ella shuffles over with difficulty to the bed, my girls still hanging off her. She hands the flowers to Maddy, brushes past her and bends down to hold the hand of the prostrate body on the bed........

Boooooom!

They say that when you die, your whole life flashes before your eyes. Take it from someone who has experience in these matters, it just isn't true. You see, your life, as you see it, is merely a series of memories that you give some kind of salient meaning to. Sights, smells, feelings, experiences. Good and bad. It is only when you weave these memories together that your story can be told. That is what life is.

I open my eyes.

====//====

====//====

I have a fresh view of the world, the weaving together of the rich tapestry of humanity and the essentialities you can't control. Human nature and the passing of time, our own shortcomings and the judgment of others, high hopes and low blows. I distil Jimmy and his northern soul; Ned and his spartan choices; Worth and his idealistic drive; Lorelei and her flight from grief; JJ's lonesome realisations; and Ella's utopian dream. I will remember them all.

They will become part of me because we are forever becoming. And we will become the rising sun.

====//====

====//====

Acknowledgements

"No Easy Way Down" - Words & Music by Gerry Goffin & Carole King

"To the Brink / Fingerprints" - Words & Music by John Bramwell & I Am Kloot

"What Went Down" - Words & Music by Foals

====//====

Don't miss out!

Click the button below and you can sign up to receive emails whenever DW Gibbs publishes a new book. There's no charge and no obligation.

https://books2read.com/r/B-A-LLMF-ADUQ

BOOKS 2 READ

Connecting independent readers to independent writers.

About the Author

David Gibbs was born in Manchester in 1968. Having worked in advertising and media for far too long, he decided it was time to try his hand at 'this writing malarky.' He now lives in Australia with his partner, Jill, and 4 children. Oh, and his dog, Lola. "How to Navigate Darkness" is his first novel.

Printed in Great Britain
by Amazon